'You'll be go
Mike said.

Erin's eyes flashed.

'Look, I have no idea of how long you're staying, but I assume the farm will be being sold and you'll be off again—'

'Taking my pound of flesh with me.'

'I didn't say that.'

'It's what you implied,' Erin said coolly. 'That I'm here for my share of my grandfather's farm. And I don't like the implication.'

'But you are just here for a holiday?' Mike demanded, his eyes meeting hers. Challenging.

Much of **Trisha David**'s childhood was spent dreaming of romance far from the Australian farming community where she lived. After marrying a fabulous doctor, she decided doctors were so sexy she could write a medical romance and has since written a considerable number under the name **Marion Lennox**. Now her vision of romance had broadened to include romances for the Enchanted™ series, and she plans to continue writing as both Marion Lennox and Trisha David.

Recent titles by the same author:

McALLISTER'S BABY

McTAVISH AND TWINS

BY
TRISHA DAVID

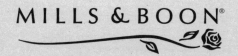

MILLS & BOON®

With thanks to Art and Kerry Uytendaal, whose knowledge
and love of horses and riding at International levels of competition
made this book possible.
This book is dedicated to Matt and Laura, who, with Bethany, Christopher
and Bryce, are now climbing my haystacks.

*First published in Great Britain 1997
Harlequin Mills & Boon Limited,
Eton House, 18-24 Paradise Road, Richmond, Surrey TW9 1SR*

© Trisha David 1997

ISBN 0 263 80364 3

*Set in Times Roman 10½ on 10¾ pt.
02-9709-53815 C1*

*Printed and bound in Great Britain
by Mackays of Chatham PLC, Chatham*

CHAPTER ONE

AUSTRALIA had the farm, Grandpa and Mike McTavish—but America was definitely safer! On the final stretch home, Erin swerved to miss two kangaroos, one snake and one fat wombat. Her final obstacle was trouble.

The twins were in the centre of the road on a blind bend. They were tiny, the suitcase between them shoulder-high, and their faces grim as death.

The children didn't flinch as Erin hit the brakes. They didn't seem to notice how close they'd come to tragedy. Instead, they tugged their suitcase sideways round her truck and trailer—and kept right on walking.

Neither child looked at Erin as she climbed from the truck. In fact both were concentrating fiercely on not looking at her.

'Hi,' Erin tried.

No response.

Erin looked dubiously down at her grubby jeans and filthy riding boots. These children were immaculately clothed in matching boy-girl outfits. They wore cute little sailor tops, with the boy in white trousers and the girl in a white skirt.

Erin looked and smelled of horse. She had to admit she seemed a great example of 'dangerous strangers'. Convincing these children to trust her was going to be hard.

'Do you two realize I nearly squashed you?' Erin demanded, raising her voice.

Still nothing. The children tugged their suitcase grimly on.

This wasn't normal kids' adventure, Erin decided,

looking at their slumped shoulders and general dejection. These children had real misery driving them.

She couldn't leave them here. They looked about six years old—certainly not old enough to be on their own. The road twisted through the hills and the next driver might not be handicapped by an ancient truck and a horse trailer. The children would have no chance against a fast car.

So Erin moved to block their path. She walked purposefully in front of them, lifted their suitcase from their grasp and hauled it over to the grass verge. Then she squatted so her eyes were on their level.

'Excuse me, but you two nearly caused an accident,' she growled softly, watching their faces for reaction. 'I had to stop so fast I might have injured my horse. You can't ignore me. It's your responsibility to at least see what damage you've done.'

Boy and girl looked at each other.

Fear receded a little. This wasn't a stranger accosting them. This was someone reminding them of their duty.

'I... We're sorry,' the little girl quavered. 'We didn't mean to...'

'That's all very well,' Erin said firmly. 'But we need to check my horse. Stay off the road while I do it.' She turned her back on the children and concentrated on opening the trailer.

Erin was almost sure Paddy was okay. Her old horse was sure-footed and calm—a veteran of years of international travel—and he'd coped with greater jolts to his trailer than this.

As Erin opened the trailer her horse swivelled to look at her with huge, reproachful eyes. His eyes almost spoke. 'Now what?' he seemed to be saying, and it was as much as Erin could do not to laugh.

'Oh, Paddy, I'm sorry.' She walked forward to stroke his nose. Another glance at the two watching children—another fast moment of thought—and then Erin shoved the ramp down and backed Paddy out onto the roadside.

Paddy clattered obediently out like the gentleman he was. He stood in the sun, gazed appreciatively at the surrounding countryside and then put his nose down to the grass and started to graze.

'He looks okay,' the little girl said doubtfully. The fear in the children's eyes had faded further, but their hands still clutched.

It was a start.

'Paddy's had a bad jolt,' Erin said firmly. 'He needs a few moments to recover.' She ran her hand affectionately over Paddy's gleaming black flank, and then along the blaze of white leading down from his wise old eyes. 'I'd like you to meet Paddy,' she said softly. 'He's my very favourite horse of all time and I'd hate anything to happen to him. And I'm Erin O'Connell. My grandpa owns a farm half a mile along this road and I'm on my way to visit him.' She smiled. 'You must live near here too.'

She paused—and waited.

'We…we don't,' the little girl said at last. 'But…but our uncle does.'

'Does he?' Erin smiled. She raised her eyebrows at the children. 'I might know him. Paddy and I have told you our names. Aren't you going to tell us yours?'

The little girl took a deep breath. She was clearly the spokesman for the two. Her brother stared numbly at Erin and his thumb moved slowly, surreptitiously towards his mouth.

'I'm Laura McTavish,' the little girl said at last. 'And this is my brother, Matthew.' She paused and then childish curiosity surfaced. 'The way you talk sounds funny…'

Laura and Matthew McTavish…

McTavish.

Erin's stomach gave a sickening lurch. Good grief! Was this some crazy coincidence?

Erin had come halfway across the world to see her grandfather, swearing all the way that she didn't have to

see Mike McTavish. Australia was a big place and she
hadn't seen Mike McTavish for ten years—not since her
last visit to Australia when she had been fourteen. She
didn't have to ask about him or have any interest in him
in any way, shape or form, she'd decided. For heaven's
sake, Mike McTavish was probably married with six
kids by now.

Maybe these were two of the brood!

Mike would be about thirty by now, Erin thought. He
was certainly old enough to be a father. He'd been
twenty when she'd seen him last, when fourteen-year-
old Erin had suffered her first and only case of puppy
love.

Unfortunately the puppy love had never quite faded.

Which was ridiculous, she told herself savagely. Her
teenage crush had been totally one-sided. Erin doubted
Mike McTavish even knew she existed, then or now.

Well… Erin shook away bitter-sweet memories with
a fierce shrug. Erin's teenage crush on Mike McTavish
was history. She forced all her attention back on the
twins.

'I'm pleased to meet you, Matthew and Laura Mc-
Tavish,' she said slowly, looking from one child to the
other, and trying not to search for a resemblance to a
ten-year-old memory. 'And I don't have a funny accent,
thank you very much. I've come all the way from the
United States of America to visit my grandpa, and every
person I've met in this country talks funny. It's not me.
It's you.'

Erin held out her hand to be shaken. The twins were
looking at Erin as if she were something newly arrived
from another planet. An American, their look said. Good
grief!

Laura was game, though. After only a moment's
hesitation the little girl solemnly took Erin's hand and
shook.

Not so her brother. One of Matthew's hands gripped
his sister so hard it must have hurt, and the other hand

was attached to a thumb being sucked like grim death. Erin smiled down at him and let her hand fall. She mustn't push too hard.

'Can I give you a lift somewhere?' Erin asked. She looked doubtfully down at their suitcase. 'It seems a very heavy load. Where are you headed?'

'No, thank you.' Laura bit her lip. 'We're going to Sydney.'

'I... I see...' Erin swallowed. She frowned. 'Laura, are you and Matthew planning to walk all the way to Sydney?'

'Yes.' Laura's voice struggled to sound defiant, but it wobbled dangerously.

'But, sweetheart, it will take you a month or more to walk that far.'

Something suspiciously like a sob broke from the little boy at Laura's side, and the little girl gulped. Her face lost its colour.

'We can do it,' she whispered. 'We...we have to. We're going home.'

'To your mom and dad?'

It was a guess, and the guess hurt. Erin had assumed the children must be holidaying here, but Laura tilted her chin and her face grew even more pale.

'Our mum and dad are dead. They were killed in a car accident.' There was no disguising the wobble in Laura's voice now. 'We're supposed to be living with Uncle Mike, but...but we don't like it and we're going home.'

Uncle Mike. Not these children's father then. Their uncle.

'To Sydney?' Erin murmured.

'Yes.'

'But... Are there different people living in your house in Sydney?' Erin queried softly, and watched the pain grow worse on both their faces.

'Yes,' Laura quavered. 'Uncle Mike says so. He says he's really sorry but our house had to be sold to someone

we don't know and we can't go back there.' A defiant
shake of her head. 'But it's our house. It's my bedroom.
Matthew's got his own room too, and Daddy painted a
yellow strip for him all the way round the ceiling just
'cos he liked it. If we go there...I mean, if we're
good...they'll have to let us stay, won't they?'

'Honey, I don't think they will,' Erin said gently.
'Laura, no matter how much they might want you to
stay, the new adults in your Sydney house will send you
straight back to your uncle Mike. They don't have a
choice, Laura. It's the law.'

'No.'

There was no point in dissembling. 'Yes,' Erin told
her. She produced a tissue and gently dried two large
tears welling from Laura's fearful eyes. 'Laura, is your
Uncle Mike really so bad you can't stay with him?'

Erin thought back to memories of Mike McTavish
from ten years ago. The man was impossibly handsome—reason enough for a fourteen-year-old to fall in
love—but he was also kind and gentle and laughing. At
twenty he'd treated life as a joke, but when Erin's grandfather had persuaded her to attend a local party Mike
McTavish had seen a strange kid's loneliness and had
come across and asked her to dance.

With the older and prettier local girls so eager for his
attention, that dance had been an act of pure kindness.
The resultant misery it had caused by tumbling Erin head
over heel in love with him was not Mike's fault.

So... Could Mike McTavish have changed so much?
Erin wondered. The Mike McTavish Erin remembered
would not—could not—treat these children with cruelty.

'He is bad!' Laura said fiercely, seeing Erin's look of
doubt. 'He is. He beats us and he doesn't feed us except
on chook food and he makes us work and work...'

'I see.' This was going from unlikely to impossible.
The corners of Erin's mouth twitched. 'Laura...'

'Y...yes?'

'Does your uncle Mike really beat you?'

Laura tried to glare but it didn't quite come off. Finally the little girl bit her lip and looked away.

Then, for the first time, Matthew spoke.

'Something worse,' the little boy whispered, hauling his thumb from his mouth. He stared at Erin as if he really needed her to understand.

'What?' The urge to gather this white-faced child in her arms and hold him close was almost overpowering but Erin fought it back.

'Aunt Caroline cut Laura's hair last night,' Matthew managed, in a choked voice that was more agonized than Laura's wildly accusing tone. 'And Uncle Mike let her.'

Silence.

Erin looked at Laura's beautifully cut bob. The little girl had fine blonde hair, gently waving. It was neat and clean and really short.

'Your uncle cut Laura's hair?'

'Aunt Caroline did,' Matthew whispered. The little boy looked at his sister's closely cropped curls with an expression of horror. 'Laura's hair was so long Daddy used to call it her mane. Mummy sat on Laura's bed every night and told us stories while she brushed Laura's hair. She said, "Always wear your hair long, Laura, because it's your crowning glory". And Aunt Caroline cut it and Uncle Mike says, "What's done's done." Now Aunt Caroline says it has to stay short all the time because it's ridiculous to keep it long. So…so we have to go… We have to go away.'

Erin flinched.

There was so much pain in the little boy's voice that Erin wanted to weep. A dull red rage was building inside her as she fought to find some way to respond. Of all the stupid, insensitive acts. Mike McTavish and the unknown, horrible Aunt Caroline had a lot to answer for. And Erin was darned if she'd defend adults who'd do such a thing.

She took a deep breath, searching for the right words. 'Your aunt and uncle were wrong to cut your hair, Laura, when it meant so much to you,' she managed. To her horror, Erin found she was choking back tears. 'But—but I don't think the answer is to run away.'

'It is!' Matthew whispered. Laura seemed too drained to speak, and it was Matthew who was now spokesman.

'No.' Finally unable to help herself, Erin reached forward to hug them both. 'And I think you know it. Your uncle is the person who looks after you now, and you need to accept that. You don't have a choice, kids. You must go home and face him—and tell him how you feel about Laura's hair.'

'We can't.' Both children stared at her, appalled.

'Well, how about if I take you?' Erin suggested softly. 'What if Paddy and I take you home and stay with you while you talk to your uncle? What if we help make him understand?'

'But she'll be there,' Laura whispered, her voice laced with revulsion. 'Aunt Caroline.'

'Paddy and I can cope with Aunt Caroline,' Erin promised. 'You see if I'm right.' She looked across at her old horse and smiled. 'We've had a lot of experience with crabby aunts. Paddy had one once who could make him turn to jelly in his horseshoes, but together we fixed her right up.'

Laura and Matthew looked at Paddy and the first trace of smiles dimpled out from the pair. 'Really? Paddy's aunt… What…what did you do?'

'We sprinkled Aunt Nobby's hay with a whole container of pepper,' Erin smiled. 'As far as we know Aunt Nobby's still sneezing.'

Matthew's pale little face creased into the beginnings of laughter.

'Could we do that to Aunt Caroline?' Laura asked breathlessly.

Erin pretended to consider—and then solemnly shook her head.

'I don't think so. I don't know how you'll make your Aunt Caroline eat hay.'

A chuckle. Then Laura gripped Erin's hand and looked down at her feet, as if figuring out a confession.

'Aunt Caroline's not really our aunt yet,' the child confided. 'But she says to call her that because she will be after she marries Mike.'

No six children. Not even a wife—yet!

'Well, there you go.' Erin smiled, shoving away such a treacherous thought. Such a useless thought! 'Caroline's not even a dinky-di aunt, and maybe if she gets to be one you could put pepper in her wedding cake. That'd fix her.'

Heaven help her if the twins really did pepper a wedding cake, Erin thought ruefully, but it was more important now to put a smile on the two small faces than to consider consequences. 'But believe me,' she added, 'Paddy and I can cope with an "almost aunt" with our hands and hooves tied behind our backs. Now…' She smiled down at both of them. 'If I promise to stay with you until no one's angry, and if I also promise to ride Paddy over and see you tomorrow, will you let me take you home?'

Matthew looked at Laura and Laura looked at Matthew. The bleakness falling back into their eyes made Erin's heart melt, but some unspoken message passed between the twins and they nodded as one.

'Okay, Erin,' Laura sighed in a voice much too old for her years. 'Matthew and I would be grateful if you'd take us h—' She caught herself. 'We'd be grateful if you could take us back to Mike's and Aunt Caroline's.'

CHAPTER TWO

MIKE MCTAVISH...

How many times had Erin said that name aloud to herself when she was fourteen? For weeks she'd been in a daze of teenage ecstasy, thinking and dreaming of nothing but Mike McTavish. She remembered saying his name as a mantra to put herself to sleep and practising her signature as Erin McTavish, Erin McTavish, Erin McTavish—but now every time Mike's name ran through her mind she was conscious of nothing but anger.

The children sat beside her in the truck as Erin drove the short distance to the McTavish farm, their eyes staring straight ahead and their expression stoic.

It would be easier to cope with tears, Erin thought grimly. This bleak resignation was breaking her heart.

What sort of hard-hearted toad had Mike McTavish become? He and his precious Caroline.

The McTavish farm was just past Erin's grandpa's.

'We're neighbours,' Erin smiled. 'That means I'll be able to see you heaps. I'm staying here for ages.'

'Why?' Laura asked, her tone implying that Erin was mad to even think of living here.

'Because my grandpa's old and he needs me,' Erin said softly. 'And I love my grandpa.'

'Not like us,' Laura said bleakly and turned away. 'We don't love anybody. Except...except each other.'

'You don't think you could love your uncle Mike?'

'We might,' Laura said bitterly. 'But he says he can't look after us on his own—so he's marrying Aunt Caroline.'

14

End of conversation. Nothing else was said until they turned into the McTavishes' gate.

Erin hadn't visited the McTavish house before, but she'd seen the house from the road and little had changed in ten years. The McTavishes were 'old money'—part of what the Australian establishment called the 'Squatocracy'. The McTavish forebears had been squatters generations ago, wealthy Britons taking up huge tracts of rich farming land and handing their wealth on to their children and their children's children.

The children's children hadn't squandered their wealth. The McTavish homestead was long and low and gracious, set in beautiful gardens with mature oaks giving blessed shade from the summer sun. It was the biggest house in the district. It was the biggest farm.

And it seemed Laura and Matthew had been missed.

As Erin's truck and trailer pulled into the yard the front door of the house burst open and a woman came striding quickly down the verandah steps towards them.

It didn't take the children's automatic bracing beside her to know this was the feared Aunt Caroline. The woman was older than Erin's twenty-four years—closer, in fact, to Mike's thirty—and somehow Caroline was just how Erin had imagined her.

Erin knew women like this. What Caroline wore was almost a uniform in upper crust rural circles—a uniform the same almost everywhere in the world.

Everything about this woman was oh-so-carefully casual. She wore designer jeans and her silk shirt fell softly open at the throat to reveal a single strand of pearls. A silk scarf casually tied back her immaculately sculpted, shoulder-length hair and her oh-so-chic sunglasses were pushed up from her beautifully made-up face.

And her face, underneath the expensive cosmetics, was cold and angry.

The woman ignored Erin. She cast one disdainful look at Erin's truck as she strode towards it, saw the children and reached up to haul the passenger door open. Matthew and Laura instinctively cringed against Erin.

'Oh, you naughty children.' The woman's voice was carefully modulated but it was razor-sharp for all that. 'Where on earth have you been? Your uncle's wasted half the morning out scouring the country and we were just about to call the police.' She fixed them with a look of dislike. 'How dare you cause us such trouble? Your uncle will be so angry!'

'Hi,' Erin said loudly across the children's heads. 'You must be Aunt Caroline. I'm Erin O'Connell.'

The woman cast Erin a look that put Erin firmly in her place—obviously way down in the animal kingdom wedged somewhere between a bedbug and a maw-worm.

'Thank you for bringing the children home,' she said briefly. She glanced at Erin again, taking in the state of Erin's clothes, and her delicate nose wrinkled in distaste. 'I suppose you want something for your trouble.'

Ugh! A tip to the lowlife...

'You're dead right I do,' Erin snapped. 'I want to see the children's uncle.'

'If you wish to see someone then you can see me,' Caroline snapped back. 'I'm their aunt.'

'Not yet, you're not.' Erin smiled her sweetest smile. Once upon a time women like this had been able to make Erin quail, but not any more. 'Until you marry their uncle I assume you're not the children's legal guardian, and that's who I need to speak to.'

The woman stared.

This was aristocratic reaction to the news that the peasants were revolting, Erin thought with grim amusement, and looked down with a rueful smile at her soiled jeans and T-shirt. In fact, Erin had to admit that this peasant was *extremely* revolting! Smelly to go with it.

It couldn't be helped. Erin waited calmly to see what the woman would say.

She never found out. There was a sudden sound of frantic barking, two collie dogs flew out from behind the machinery shed to investigate the strange truck on their property—and behind them strode Mike McTavish.

Mike stopped dead when he saw the truck, and as the farmer saw Laura and Matthew in the cab Erin saw his face slacken with relief.

As Erin's face froze…

Mike McTavish…

Erin stared, and somewhere around her heart she felt a sickening jolt. It seemed that the ghost of fourteen-year-old Erin still had the power to hurt.

Mike McTavish was just the same as Erin remembered—only more so!

The farmer had the build of someone who pumped weights, but this man hadn't built his muscles in a sweaty gymnasium. He'd built his muscles from heaving hay-bales and working constantly on the land. The McTavishes had money, Erin knew, but this man obviously didn't sit back and expect the hired help to do his hard work for him.

He was older, of course—ten years more mature than the Mike McTavish she remembered. His face had become weathered from a life spent outdoors, and the hard-working image was deepened by the rough moleskins, open-necked khaki shirt and heavy work boots he wore.

Erin blinked and blinked again as her heart gave the same lurch she remembered. She still remembered the sensation when a youthful version of this man had walked across the dance floor—all those years ago.

Mike was still blatantly good-looking. His deep brown unkempt hair showed traces of bleaching from the harsh Australian sun and his farmer's eyes were creased from the same bright glare—but he was still the same Mike McTavish…

For heaven's sake, get a hold on yourself, Erin told herself harshly. Somehow she forced herself to move, jumping down from the truck and moving swiftly round so she was between children and both uncle and aunt.

'Mr McTavish,' she said softly, ignoring the horrible Caroline completely and holding out her hand.

Mike stopped five feet from Erin. He stared, his dark eyes taking in Erin from the tip of her stable-mired boots to her roughly tied back mass of chestnut curls.

'I don't think I know you,' he said slowly.

I'm not sure I want to, his gaze seemed to imply, and Erin flushed. He showed not the least sign of recognition, and that in itself hurt. She could cope with Caroline's nasty tongue more easily than this man's frank uninterest.

She caught herself, fighting down a mounting blush. Mike McTavish's gaze had moved past her to the children in the truck. Ignoring Erin's extended hand, he took a step forward. But Erin would have none of it. Her body blocked his path.

'Mr McTavish, I'm Erin O'Connell…'

Mike's attention was no longer on Erin at all. It was all on the children.

'Laura…Matt…are you okay? You're not hurt?' His voice was hoarse with worry.

And in that moment Erin forgave Mike McTavish for not recognizing her. There was sheer, raw anxiety in the farmer's desperate question, and she realized he'd ignored her solely from concern for the twins.

Neither child answered. Mike was looking straight past Erin, practically pressing against her, and it took all Erin's resolve to continue blocking his path.

'They're fine,' Erin told Mike quickly, glancing back at the children's white little faces. Her body was hard against the open passenger door and Mike McTavish was so darned close… 'They're just tired, stressed and—and very, very unhappy.'

Mike's gaze carefully studied both children, searching their faces himself for assurance that what Erin had said was true.

Finally he looked back down to Erin, his extra height making her feel tiny.

'Who did you say you were?' he demanded, finally reassured she was telling the truth. He took a step back—but he was still too close. 'You sound… American.'

'Half-American, half-Australian.' Erin smiled. 'I'm Erin O'Connell. My grandpa owns the farm next door.'

'O'Connell…' Mike's brow cleared, relief deepening. This was a relative of a neighbour, bringing his children home. Not so bad after all. He looked at her more closely. 'Did they…? Were they on your place?'

'They were two miles down the road,' Erin told him, her smile fading. 'Walking dead centre of the road on a blind curve. I nearly hit them.'

Mike flinched. The farmer closed his eyes, as if in pain. Beside him, the woman called Caroline had grown silent, her eyes cool and watchful.

Finally Mike McTavish opened his eyes and looked down at Erin again.

'Thank you,' he said softly, and the gentleness Erin remembered so well was there in force. He smiled, a weary smile that still had the power to light his eyes. 'Thank you,' he repeated, and his eyes smiled directly into hers with all the warmth Erin had carried in her heart for so long. 'For driving carefully and for bringing them home safely.' He shook his head, wondering. 'I drove down the lanes round here looking for them, but I couldn't believe they'd gone so far. I decided they must be trying to cut across paddocks, so I've had the farm bike out searching cross-country.'

'They were very determined,' Erin said. 'They tell me they were making for Sydney.'

Once again there was a look of raw pain flashing across Mike's face.

'Of course.' His eyes still held hers but any trace of a smile was completely gone. 'Sydney was their home before—before my brother and his wife were killed. But they can't go back.'

'The twins explained that to me.' Erin was acutely

conscious of the children behind her, listening to every
word. She'd promised the children she'd speak up for
them and they were waiting for her to carry out her
promise.

So do it, she told herself firmly, searching for the right
words. Just do it!

'I believe both the children understand their home's
been sold,' she continued finally, her soft voice tremu-
lous in the farmyard stillness. 'But they were desperate.'

'Desperate?' Mike's face was confused.

'The children ran away because you cut Laura's hair,'
Erin managed. For some reason it was difficult to get
each word out—it was so desperately important to make
Mike see the children's hurt. 'Their parents loved
Laura's hair and told her she should leave it long. Last
night you cut it. Both Laura and Matthew felt it more
than if you'd beaten them. I believe—I believe you were
wrong to cut it. I think you owe Laura an apology, and
if she wants to grow her hair long again she should have
your full support.'

Caroline's breath hissed in.

'That's ridiculous,' the woman whispered, casting an
uncertain glance at Mike. 'What gives you the right…?'

'What gives you the right?' Erin demanded, her eyes
flashing fire. If she couldn't hug these children as she
wanted, at least she could fight their battles for them.
'Laura didn't want her hair cut. Would it have hurt so
much to leave it long?'

'Michael has enough to do in the mornings without
combing the b…the child's hair.'

'Were you going to say brat?' Erin asked slowly.

'No.' It was Mike again, his voice heavy. He placed
a hand on Caroline's silk-clad shoulder, stilling her with
the gesture. 'Of course she wasn't.' He sighed. 'How do
you know all this?' he asked Erin, and the pain was still
in his voice.

'The twins told me,' Erin said gently. 'They told me

when I asked. I think—I think they're desperate to have an adult on—on their side.'

It was a direct hit and it went home hard. Mike winced.

'Caroline meant this for the best,' he said slowly, his eyes flicking into the truck to the twins. 'Laura's hair has been tangled and I don't cope with it very well. I can't make it look like her mother did.'

'Does that matter so much?'

'I guess…' Mike stared helplessly down at her, a man right out of his depth.

Erin gave a rueful smile. This situation needed cheering up—fast. It was altogether too grim for words.

Okay. So think fast, Erin, she told herself.

And her smile deepened as she figured what to do.

She did a half-pirouette so that she had her back to the big farmer and she was facing the twins. She gave them both a reassuring wink. 'My hair took ten seconds to brush this morning,' she confessed, still with her back and her wayward ponytail to Mike. 'It's tied back with a bit of hay band. Is it so bad?'

She smiled at the twins again, pirouetted back to face Mike McTavish and tilted her chin, defying him with her eyes.

The farmer's grim expression faded. Mike McTavish's lips twitched. His eyes took in Erin's disreputable hair, her dancing eyes, and then slowly took in the rest of her.

It was as if he was seeing Erin for the first time—and his eyes told her he very much liked what he saw.

'I guess…I guess it doesn't look too bad,' he said slowly, and his eyes reflected her laughter.

'Laura could do her hair this way all by herself,' Erin said firmly. She pirouetted again to face the children and twinkled. 'Couldn't you, Laura? Matt could tie it for you. I bet you could even persuade Aunt Caroline to buy you some ribbon instead of hay band. If you grow your hair long again, Laura, would you mind if it's as messy as mine?'

Both children gazed at Erin, considering. Erin's hair was certainly not beautifully groomed. It was a mass of chestnut curls, escaping from her hay band in errant wisps all over her face.

'I like it,' Matthew said finally, removing his thumb and casting a scared, defiant look at Caroline.

'It's got straw in it.' Laura managed a smile. 'And…and I think there's a bit of dry horse dung stuck at the back. But it still looks pretty.'

'There.' Erin's eyes danced with laughter. She faced Mike again. 'Even with horse dung, your problem's solved.'

'But Michael doesn't want the children looking like tramps,' Caroline snapped, fury getting the better of her.

Erin's laughter faded—and slowly she turned to face Caroline's hostility head-on. 'Is that what I look like?'

'Since you ask, yes. You look like you haven't washed for weeks.'

'Caroline…' Mike's grip on Caroline's shoulder tightened, and his face closed as if he'd like to haul back the words his fiancée had spoken.

They were impossible to haul back.

There was a moment's dreadful silence. Mike and the twins all looked as though they expected Erin to explode—and then Erin's lips twitched again as her sense of the ridiculous sprang to her rescue.

'I've met a few tramps who'd take personal affront at the comparison with messy me.' She smiled, allaying Mike's dismay with her chuckle. Her eyes danced up at his. 'I doubt if horse dung's everyone's ideal hair decor. But it doesn't matter. I've spent most of this morning mucking out stables.'

She faced Caroline again and managed to maintain her smile in spite of the woman's transparent disdain. 'I'd love to wear silk scarves and pearls to work,' she smiled.

'But I just bet my horse would try to eat them. You must have a more appreciative audience than I have.'

Caroline's jaw dropped about a foot.

The woman sure didn't have a sense of humour. The look Caroline was directing at Erin said plainly that she thought Erin was mocking her. She thought the lowlife was thumbing its nose at its social betters!

Well, maybe she shouldn't have commented on Caroline's appearance, Erin thought ruefully. It just sort of slipped out before she could stop it.

So behave yourself, Erin, she told herself firmly. Be careful.

Then she hesitated. Erin blocked out Caroline's transparent fury as she considered how to make her point to Mike. This was important.

She tilted her chin yet again and met his look with defiance, a half-smile returning to her lips. It was a smile of entreaty.

'If I'd stopped to shower and change clothes, I would have been late for my grandpa and made him worried— as I'm worrying him now,' she said softly. 'I didn't do that. But the kids are important. These two are worth worrying Grandpa for. It's all…it's all a matter of priority. How important is it to you that Laura is immaculate?'

'It's not,' Mike said softly.

And then, before Erin knew what he was about, she was lifted by the waist by Mike's strong hands and moved bodily aside. Mike leaned into the cab and gathered the two frightened children into his arms. His broad shoulders accommodated them both with ease as he lifted them clear.

'You heard what Erin said, kids,' he told them gently. 'Erin's grandpa is worried because she's late, so we'll let her go.' He turned to Erin again, the children held tight in his arms. 'Thank you again for bringing them home, but we'll take care of them now,' he said softly. 'Believe me.'

Erin met his look. She took a deep breath. 'I promised—I promised I wouldn't leave here unless I knew no one would be angry with the children.'

'No one's angry,' Mike said gently, holding them close. 'Are we, Caroline?'

Caroline sure was. She'd clearly enjoy horsewhipping the American lowlife at the very least, but the look on Mike McTavish's face checked her. With a discernible effort the woman forced herself to speak.

'Of course not. I mean—not at the children.' She cast Erin a look of glittering dislike.

'Laura will be permitted to grow her hair?' Erin demanded. If ever she was going to achieve something for the twins, now was the time.

'Of course she can,' Mike said heavily. He cast an unsure glance at Caroline. 'Caroline…I mean, *we* thought we were acting for the best, but maybe…maybe we should have talked it over first.'

There was no mistaking the reproof behind the words, and Caroline didn't like it one bit.

'That's just fine.' Erin smiled before Caroline could answer. She walked round to the driver's door of her truck and hesitated. 'I also promised the twins I'd ride over and see them tomorrow. Is that okay?'

'There's no need…' Caroline was almost speechless.

'There is a need,' Erin said firmly. 'I promised.'

'Of course you can come.' Mike was almost totally occupied with his armload of children but he flashed her a smile that held. It was exactly the same smile that had knocked Erin's socks off all those years ago. 'You'll be very welcome.'

Erin flashed a look at Caroline's livid face.

'I'll just bet I won't be.' She smiled ruefully. 'But I'll come just the same.'

CHAPTER THREE

ERIN'S grandpa was just where she'd left him ten years ago.

She turned into the driveway of O'Connell's farm and looked up to see Jack O'Connell lazily rocking back and forth in his favourite chair on the verandah.

It was like coming home.

Erin beeped the horn as a deep contentment welled up inside her. The events of the past hour faded. She was going to miss her parents so much it hurt—miss home and miss the life she'd built herself—but the decision to come here was the right one. The only one. She had been talking of it for so long—and finally she was here.

Why was this place so special?

The O'Connell place didn't hold a candle to the McTavishes'. The farm itself was maybe a tenth of the size of the neighbouring landholding, and the small weatherboard cottage looked ramshackle in comparison.

Where the McTavishes had manicured gardens and English oaks and elms, here the paddocks ran right up to the verandah. Fat cattle wandered up to the windows or lazed in the shade of the gum trees round the house. Compared to the McTavishes it was definitely a poor relation—though not quite an abode fit for tramps!

This tramp was content, Erin thought happily. Her grandpa's farm looked a million dollars to Erin. Home is where the heart is, and Erin's heart had been split in two since her visit here ten years ago. Half was in America and half was here—but, by coming here, maybe the two halves could be brought closer together.

On the verandah the old man had stopped his rocking,

25

his gnarled, weather-beaten face crinkling into a broad beam of welcome. Jack O'Connell came slowly down the verandah steps, but he hadn't reached the bottom before Erin was flying up to meet him.

'Grandpa…'

'Erin… Erin, love… Well, well…' Jack O'Connell hugged his granddaughter hard and then held her at arm's length. 'Let me look at you.'

'Let me look at you!' Erin was laughing and weeping in his arms. 'Oh, Grandpa…'

He was the same Grandpa. Jack O'Connell was older and infinitely more worn—heavens, he was near eighty now, Erin thought with dismay—but there was life and vigour in the old face yet.

'Eh, you're the spitting image of your mother,' Jack said softly. 'It's good to have you here, Erin lass.'

'It's good to be here.' Erin tucked her arm through her grandpa's and led him back up to the verandah. 'Now all that's left for us to do is to catch up on ten years' gossip.' She grinned. 'But we have all the time in the world to do it.'

'All the time in the world…?'

'I'm here to stay, Grandpa,' Erin said firmly. 'So you'd better get used to me.'

'Tell me about Mike McTavish,' Erin ventured over her third cup of tea and Jack's first beer.

The shadows were lengthening from the towering gum trees, and soon it would be time for dinner, but neither Erin nor Jack felt like moving. There was a deep satisfaction in them both, and as they talked Erin saw the lines of strain she'd noticed in her grandfather's face slowly start to fade. Already he seemed somehow younger.

It must have been so hard for this man to watch his only son migrate to America, she thought. Erin's dad had had his own hard reasons for moving his family to the United States and Jack knew and approved—but

Jack had been left alone too long. Erin's decision to return was the right decision.

'What do you want to know about Mike McTavish?' Jack asked cautiously. He cast a slightly anxious look at Erin. 'The lad's engaged to be married, Erin.'

Erin winced as she saw his anxious look. So Jack O'Connell had noticed his granddaughter's childish crush ten years ago! Oh, dear! If grandpa had noticed, it must have been obvious to everyone.

The only consolation was that it hadn't been memorable to Mike McTavish. Mike McTavish seemed not even to remember her. Which was just as well...

'Grandpa, I'm a grown lady now.' Erin smiled, even though the smile cost her an effort. 'You can put what I was like when I was fourteen right out of your mind.'

Jack grinned affectionately across at his grand-daughter. 'Well, you sure were stuck on Mike McTavish.' He hesitated. 'It did cross my mind...when I had your letter saying you were coming...' He shook his head. 'Your parents look like staying in Pittsburgh for a lifetime now. Your mother tells me your dad will never be fit enough to travel. So...what made you come back?'

'It wasn't because of Mike McTavish,' Erin said soundly. She hesitated. 'Or maybe...' She met her grandfather's look, fair and square. 'Maybe it was, in a way. Because when Mom and Dad sent me out to visit you ten years ago, I had that awful crush.' She smiled self-consciously. 'And, I'll admit, for a while there I dreamed of marrying the man. Fourteen-year-olds are like that. But it started me thinking what it would be like to live here for ever. And somehow...somehow it wouldn't go away. The feeling that here was home.'

'Your parents moved away when you were five,' Jack growled. 'This is hardly home.'

'It is,' Erin insisted. 'It's Pittsburgh that's never seemed home to me.' She bit her lip. 'Grandpa, I don't like the city. You know I've spent every minute I can on farms. I did an agricultural course in the States—'

'In between riding horses.'

'In between horses,' she agreed. 'But I always knew
this was where I wanted to be. It's my dad's home. And
all of us have hated you being here by yourself.'

'Your parents approved of your coming?'

'Even Mom.' Erin smiled. 'She's married to an Aussie
and she's resigning herself to having an Aussie daughter.'

'But your riding…'

'I can ride here.'

'Not—'

'Grandpa, it doesn't matter.' Erin reached out and
took his hand. 'I want to live here. It's my decision.'

'And…and Mike McTavish had nothing to do with
it?'

Erin shook her head and smiled. 'Honest, Grandpa. It
has nothing to do with Mike McTavish.' Or, at any rate,
she acknowledged to herself, not very much.

Jack O'Connell smiled, as if suspecting Erin's mild
deception. His crinkled old eyes saw heaps. They always
had. 'So why are you asking about Mike McTavish then,
lass?' he asked gently. 'If you haven't been thinking of
him.'

'Because I've already met him again…'

Briefly Erin outlined the events of the afternoon. Jack
O'Connell listened in silence and then nodded slowly to
himself.

'I'll bet Mike McTavish won't have known about the
child's hair until it was cut,' he said slowly. 'Mike's a
good lad. He wouldn't hurt a child deliberately and it's
local opinion he's nutty on the twins. No. The hair-
cutting sounds just like Caroline Podger.'

'Tell me about Caroline.' Erin nestled down in her
ancient chair, contented. Jack O'Connell had always
been a man of few words—but one who saw a lot for
all his silence. He told no one his troubles but he seemed
to know the troubles of everyone else.

Jack shrugged. 'I can't tell you much, girl. Only what I've heard on the grapevine.'

'That'll do me,' Erin said promptly. 'I seem to remember you having the best grapevine of anyone I know.'

'Cheeky…' He smiled, his old eyes drinking his granddaughter in.

'So go on. Tell me.'

'Caroline Podger…' Jack nodded. 'Well, the girl's family have a big place north of here, I gather. They're not much liked. Her dad treats his employees like dirt and then whinges round the district because he can't get good help. Word is, his daughter's worse than her old man. Rumour is she has a vicious temper, but she keeps it well hidden from those she considers important. Like Mike McTavish.'

'Have they been engaged long?' Erin asked, consciously trying to keep her voice sounding uninterested.

Jack threw her a look which said he wasn't fooled in the least. 'Three months,' he told her. He shrugged. 'Mike's been on his own since his dad died. His older brother had no taste for farming and moved to Sydney— then got himself and his wife killed. Those two little kiddies landed on Mike's doorstep the day after.' He grimaced. 'That put paid to Mike McTavish's bachelor existence right there and then.'

'He…' Erin bit her lip. How to ask? 'Mike's had a few girlfriends?'

'Well, I've heard he likes the ladies, does our Mike.' Jack grinned. 'Can't say I blame him. I did the same once, before I met your grandmother. Still, when your grandma came along I was fair smitten—but Mike seems to have chosen his bride because of her suitability.'

'Suitability?'

'They move in the same circles,' Jack told her. 'They've been an on-again off-again item for years. It always seemed to the district they just used each other as a social convenience between more interesting partners—but suddenly it's more than that. She's getting long in the tooth—and he wants a wife.

'Caroline's groomed herself well for the job. She's done a cordon bleu cookery course or some such thing in France. She makes a wonderful hostess and as a social organizer she's second to none. Mike McTavish lived a pretty messy bachelor existence until the twins. So... he's made up his mind to marry a lady trained for the job.' He grimaced. 'Can't say I'd like to wake up next to *that* every morning, though.'

'But...Grandpa, surely he must...well, he must love her. To ask her to marry him...'

'Folk say he panicked,' Jack said slowly. 'And who's to blame him—a single man saddled with two grief-stricken six-year-olds out of the blue? Maybe anyone would have panicked in the same circumstances. Grace Brown does housework for him two mornings a week, but she has her own husband and boys and farm to run. Domestic help here is darned hard to find. For Mike McTavish—a lad who doesn't know one thing about raising kids—our Caroline must have seemed a sensible solution.

'And maybe she's just as pragmatic. Word is that her father's running short on money; she's not trained for a lot beside social niceties and Mike's offer must have looked as good to her as it seemed sensible to him.'

'Ugh.'

Erin shuddered and Jack O'Connell subjected his granddaughter to a long, scrutinizing stare.

'What the squatocracy do with their lives isn't our business, though, Erin girl,' Jack said softly. His gaze grew a little anxious. 'Now... You did say...you did say you were staying a while?'

'If you'll have me.' Erin hesitated and then took his hand. 'Your last letter said you're thinking of selling.'

'I don't have a choice,' her grandpa said roughly. 'I can't manage the place on my own any more.' He looked out over the lush green pastures to the rolling hills beyond. This area of the western district of Victoria, with its rich river plains and scattered red gum trees was arguably one of the most beautiful parts of Australia. 'It'll break my heart, though, lass,' he whispered. 'I don't mind admitting it.'

'Well, that's why I'm here.' Erin caught his hand. 'Grandpa, you know I love this place. You know I always have. I've done two years' agricultural training between my mucking about with horses. I've been working part-time as farm hand and horse strapper since I left home. And all I want...' She took a deep breath. 'All I want from life is to live here and run this farm for you. For us. What do you say, Grandpa? Could you bear to have me?'

The old man's eyes filled with tears. He put a hand up to shove them away but more welled up after them.

'You wouldn't be bored silly?' he managed in a choked voice.

'I promise.'

'There's not much social life round here.'

'I don't need social life.'

'But...a girl like you should be going to parties. Enjoying yourself. Meeting young men and getting married.'

Erin shook her head.

'Not me, Grandpa,' she said softly. 'Believe me. I don't need anyone. I don't need anything. Only you and Paddy and this farm.'

'You're crazy,' the old man whispered, a smile wavering out between tears.

'Crazy or not, if you'll have me I'm staying.'

Erin slept soundly in the same bed she'd slept in as a teenager. She was woken at dawn by magpies and kookaburras, and when she flung open the window to greet the day she was met by a huge Hereford cow. The creature shoved her nose in and inspected Erin's pyjama-clad figure with interest.

'Ugh…' Laughing and supremely content, Erin shoved the nose back outside. 'Introductions later, ma'am.'

Still laughing, she showered and dressed fast and made her way outside.

Breakfast took ages. Jack O'Connell was almost absurdly anxious that she'd changed her mind in the night, but was intent, nevertheless, on telling her the worst.

There was a small voice at the back of Erin's head telling her she wanted to spend the morning visiting the twins—and their uncle—but on that first morning Jack went through the farm figures with her.

Erin blocked the McTavishes from her thoughts and listened with care. This was important. This was her future life. As she went slowly through the books she was never more grateful for her farm management training.

There were things wrong here that needed to be faced, but there was nothing insurmountable. By the end of the morning there was hope in both their faces. Jack and Erin ate a companionable lunch, both immeasurably cheered, and then Jack disappeared for an afternoon nap. Finally Erin let her inner voice hold sway. She went to saddle Paddy.

'Your first gallop on an Australian farm,' she said fondly to the horse as she saddled him. 'I hope you like it, Pad. I think we're here to stay.'

She should be checking Jack's stock, she thought as she and Paddy finally rode east across the paddocks towards the McTavishes. From here the Hereford herd looked lazy, well fed and contented, but, by the look of the books, Erin knew there were problems. Grandpa hadn't got round to drenching this year, and his calving had been a disaster.

There was also the little matter of the hay…

The problems would have to wait. Erin's inner voice was fair screaming at her now. It was a case of priorities again, she told herself. Laura and Matthew were top of the list.

The fact that she'd see Mike McTavish again had nothing to do with it!

The twins were waiting for her—two small urchins hanging over the gate—and their matching grins as Erin and Paddy appeared over the rise made Erin grin herself. What a difference! This was certainly a change from yesterday.

'We've been waiting and waiting,' Laura announced importantly. 'Since crack of dawn!'

'Crack!' Erin whistled, impressed. 'Wow!'

'Mike says we have to tell him as soon as you arrive—and we asked Mrs Brown to make scones before she went home. All we have to do is stick them in the oven and they'll take twelve minutes.' Both children regarded Erin anxiously, as if she might dig her heels into Paddy's flanks and gallop off. 'You can stay twelve minutes, can't you?'

'Of course I can,' Erin smiled, dismounting. 'For fresh scones, I could stay an hour.'

They hardly heard. Their matching whoops of delight filled the yard as both children screamed off towards the house.

'Uncle Mike...Mike, she's here. Mike...'

The title seemed to be dropped at will, Erin thought, noting that the children were more accustomed to just plain 'Mike' than 'Uncle Mike'. It seemed a healthy sign. With Aunt Caroline there was no such dropping of the guard.

'Mike... She's here, Mike, and she's brought Paddy.'

The children were pretending to be aeroplanes, Erin figured, watching them swoop their arms and veer from side to side as they ran. Two happy, healthy, normal six-year-olds. The change from yesterday was amazing.

Ten seconds later they reappeared from the house, each towing the unfortunate Mike's hand. Whatever their uncle had been doing had clearly been deemed unimportant.

Mike was laughing, though. A willing prisoner…

'Now, you stay and talk to Erin,' Laura bossed importantly, towing her uncle close and abandoning him. 'Matthew and I have to fix the scones.' She hesitated. 'But you'll come in and take them out of the oven when we yell, won't you?' she asked anxiously. 'Mrs Brown said we weren't allowed to do that ourselves.'

'I sure will.' Mike ruffled Laura's hair before sending both aeroplanes winging back across the yard. He watched them go with affection and then turned to Erin. The smile Erin knew so well creased his face.

'Thank you for coming.' He smiled. 'The twins were counting on it.'

His smile deepened—and locked. And then faded as if Mike McTavish was suddenly unsure.

'I…I promised.'

'So you did.'

There was no sign of Caroline. The relief of not having to face the supercilious woman was making Erin feel light-headed; Mike McTavish had always had the power to make her feel different. Special.

'Would you like to let Paddy loose to graze? There's a small paddock behind the sheds.' With a perceptible effort Mike shifted his gaze to Paddy.

'No.' Erin fought to make her voice less breathless. 'I'll just hitch him…'

'You're not staying long?'

'Long enough for some scones.' Still the same stupid breathlessness.

'Paddy's a great horse.'

Mike McTavish's voice seemed almost as constrained as Erin's. Both of them were focusing their attention on the horse to take off the pressure. Mike ran a hand over Paddy's gleaming flank. Erin had groomed him for half an hour before saddling him and it showed, his jet-black coat shining like velvet. The farmer stood back and looked at the gleaming thoroughbred, assessing him carefully. 'He looks…he looks almost as if he could have been a racehorse.'

'He's an old steeplechaser,' Erin told him, her eyes starting to smile again. Any talk of Paddy made her smile. 'Well—he was a would-be steeplechaser. He moves like the wind in training, but, given a line-up of horses on a track, Paddy stops dead and waits for the others to disappear. He likes the attention all to himself, does my Paddy.'

There was no disguising the affection in Erin's voice, and Mike looked across at her curiously.

His gaze unsettled her.

Well, if he was assessing Erin as well as Paddy, at least she wasn't quite as disreputable as yesterday, Erin decided nervously as Mike's eyes raked her slim body. She was still clad in jeans and T-shirt but her hair was neatly brushed and tied back with a scarf, and she was almost clean.

Almost. She couldn't be immaculate after spending half an hour grooming a dusty horse.

'You are American,' Mike said slowly as he looked at her. 'Your accent…'

'It's not much of one,' Erin said defensively, and flushed.

'It's definitely not Australian.'

'If I've lost my Aussie drawl I'm happy,' she smiled. 'But I'd prefer not to sound too broadly American.'

'I think your speech is a mixture of both.' Mike grinned. 'I wouldn't worry. It's attractive…'

Oh, great. Erin had come a long way, then. Fourteen years ago she'd been nothing but a gawky kid. Now at least she had an attractive accent!

'I've been trying to figure you out.' Mike took Paddy's reins from her and led him over to the trough beside the verandah. This place was well set up for horses. 'Erin O'Connell… I didn't think Jack had any relatives in the country.'

'He has me.' Her voice sounded a bit breathless.

'He hasn't seen much of you,' Mike said slowly. 'He's been pretty neglected these last few years.'

There was an edge of criticism in his tone and Erin flushed.

'I would have come before,' she said softly, not meeting his eye. 'But it wasn't possible.'

'You must be Jack's son's daughter?'

'Yes.'

'I thought I recognized you,' he said slowly. 'Jack's son left for America almost twenty years ago and Jack never talks about him. But you…you came back to visit when you were a kid…'

'That's right.'

'I vaguely remember. But that was just you.' Mike's brow was still creased in thought. 'It hasn't been possible for your father to visit?' There was no mistaking the implied criticism now, and Erin found her temper rising to match his tone.

'No.'

'Money's a problem, then, is it?'

Whew… Erin took a hasty step back. Michael McTavish's tone had been sardonic, and Erin's temper moved from simmering to hiss of steam. If he knew the real reason…

She was darned if she'd tell him. Sympathy was one thing she didn't want from this man.

'Our family's finances are none of your business, Mike McTavish…' She took a deep breath, searching for control. 'But you shouldn't have to ask. I'd imagine you can guess. Tramps don't earn enough to fund overseas travel.'

'Ouch!'

Mike blinked at the flaming virago before him and his eyes slowly crinkled into a lazy, self deprecating smile. '*Touché*, Miss O'Connell.' The sarcasm in his voice disappeared and his smile deepened. 'I guess, despite your neglect of your grandpa, I do owe you an apology for yesterday. Caroline was overwrought. She'd been very worried.'

'I could see that,' Erin agreed, her temper still simmering. 'Out scouring paddocks with you, was she? Or sitting by the phone, frantic with anxiety?'

It was Mike's turn to glower then. The easy smile slipped.

'You've a sharp tongue.'

'It's my bad upbringing,' Erin said softly. 'I didn't go to the right schools.'

'Oh, for heaven's sake...' Mike spread his hands. He sighed. 'Look, Miss O'Connell, can we call a truce? It's too nice a day for World War Three and the twins are cooking scones. Come on into the house and we'll see how they're going.'

'Do you have a tradesman's entrance?' Erin muttered, and Mike's expression of exasperation deepened.

'Miss O'Connell...'

'Sir!'

'Erin, shut up!'

She glowered some more, but couldn't quite maintain it. Her eyes peeped up at him and a twinkle lurked in their clear green depths.

He saw it.

'You're laughing at me,' he said slowly.

'Me? Laugh at you?' Erin tugged an imaginary forelock. 'Oh, please, sir, no, sir. I never could, sir. Not in a million years. I know my place, sir.'

'Erin?'

'Yes, sir?'

'If you don't shut up and come and eat some scones, your place will be at the bottom of the duck pond. I believe that was the remedy for harping women in times when the lower order knew their place.'

'The ducking stool or nothing.' She grinned. 'But it will have been worth it. To harp or not to harp...' She was feeling light-headed and silly and it showed. It was a glorious day. She was finally where she wanted to be—

in Australia again after all these years. The horrid
Caroline was nowhere to be seen and all seemed right
with her world.

'You're nuts, Erin O'Connell,' Mike McTavish said
slowly, staring down at her with the beginnings of laughter in his eyes.

'You've only just noticed that?' Erin smiled up at him.
'Well, Mr McTavish…sir…' She bobbed a mock curtsey. 'You ain't seen nothin' yet!'

What followed was a very happy half-hour. Mike and
Erin's conversation degenerated into silliness and the
twins joined in with relish.

'Now, best manners, please, you lot,' Mike ordered as
he and Erin entered the kitchen. 'You know how
Australia and England and Canada all have the same
Queen?'

'Yes?' Both twins gazed at their uncle, bemused.

'Well, this lady's from America.' Mike grinned. 'And
the Americans were so rude about paying for some tea
a long time ago that the Queen didn't want them any
more. So…it's up to us to teach her manners—show her
we're brought up properly in the Antipodes.'

The twins glanced nervously from Erin to Mike—and
slowly relaxed. They didn't understand what Mike was
talking about but they could sense laughter in their big
uncle and they were all too ready to join in.

The twins and the unknown Mrs Brown had excelled
themselves. The scones were light, fluffy and delicious.
There was a vast bowl of farm cream to go with them
and strawberry jam tasting of strawberries straight from
the garden.

'Mrs Brown made strawberry jam last Monday,'
Laura told Erin importantly, helping herself to a fourth
scone. 'We helped.'

'I hope you stayed clean all the time,' Erin smiled.
Then she caught herself. It was okay to mock Mike

McTavish—but not the children. To her delight, though, Laura giggled.

'We didn't,' Laura admitted. 'Mrs Brown said we looked like two Indian warriors in war paint after we'd finished. She tossed us into the bath, clothes and all.'

Erin smiled back and then, because she couldn't help herself, she added another question.

'Doesn't Caroline come on Mondays either?'

Silence.

Matthew slowly shook his head and both children stared down at their plates.

Then, as one, the twins pushed back their plates and rose.

'We'll meet you outside,' Laura said. 'We'll go and pat Paddy.'

The message was plain: if you intend to speak about Caroline, we're off.

The door slammed behind them and Erin slowly turned back to Mike.

'I'm sorry…'

His laughter had faded as well.

'I'll thank you not to do that,' he said savagely. 'Criticizing Caroline in front of the children…'

'I hardly criticized her,' Erin muttered. 'I only asked if she came on Mondays.'

'You know exactly what you did.'

'Yes.' Erin stood up, gathering plates and carrying them across to the sink. This man wasn't her social better, even though he had more money. He wasn't even twenty years old any more, to her gawky fourteen years. She owed him nothing—and it was time he heard the truth. She turned back to face him, leaning against the bench with the table between them. 'I know what I did. I inferred the twins don't have fun when Caroline's around. But it's true, isn't it?'

'No.'

'No?' Erin shrugged. 'They seem scared stiff of her if you ask me.'

'Only because she disciplines them,' Mike said slowly. 'With me...with me they run wild. Laura especially. Matt just goes silent—sometimes for days on end—and I worry about him. I can't seem to get through to the kid.'

He spread his hands. 'Do you have any idea how difficult it is, Miss O'Connell, to be thrown in at the deep end as parent to two grief stricken six-year-olds? You've no idea, have you? I had to fly up to Sydney and collect them from their babysitter the night their parents were killed. I was at a bucks' party when the call came. To be catapulted like that...'

He sighed and spread his hands. 'Look, I'm doing my best, but I'm not a parent. Caroline takes on that role and I'm grateful to her. She makes sure they're respectable and well disciplined and...and safe, and I'd be mad if I sat here and let you criticize her. We're both doing what we can in a very difficult situation, Miss O'Connell, and your interference isn't helping one bit.'

'So I should have left them on the road yesterday? I should have driven right on?'

'That's not what I mean and you know it.'

'It is what you mean in a sense,' Erin said slowly. 'You're saying I should butt out of what's not my business, and if I'd done that then I would have driven on yesterday instead of stopping.' She took a deep breath. 'It's not in my nature to drive on through,' she said softly. 'I just can't.'

'It might not be in your nature but it's in your blood,' Mike said harshly. 'Your family left your grandfather twenty years ago, and as far as I know there's only been the one visit since.'

Erin's chin tilted. 'That's right.' She met his look. 'I was sent out from America at fourteen.'

'I do vaguely remember you,' he admitted. 'All steel braces and freckles.' He smiled. 'The freckles haven't changed.' Then he looked at her a little more searchingly. 'If you're the kid I remember—I thought of you as a loner. An unhappy, solitary sort of kid. Are you an only child?'

'Yes.'

'And your parents sent you out by yourself.' He grimaced. 'It can't have been much fun.'

'You're judging my father, aren't you?' Erin said softly. 'You have him all summed up. A man who leaves his father and goes halfway round the world without a backward glance. A man who sends his teenage daughter overseas on her own as a sop to his conscience—once and never again.'

'Look, there may be reasons I don't know...'

'There are,' Erin said dully. 'If you'd asked my grandfather, then maybe you would have found out.'

'Your grandfather doesn't talk of his family,' Mike told her. 'We've been neighbours for a long time—but when I ask about his family he clams up. He's been so darned lonely, though. He's been just plain miserable for the past couple of years as his health has failed, and there's pain comes into his eyes whenever anyone asks about his family. I can sense how much he misses family, and maybe that's why I'm sounding so judgemental.'

'You've no right...'

'Well, if you don't want me judging, then maybe you should answer some questions.' Mike's dark eyes didn't leave Erin's face. 'Why no contact for so long and then, a month or so after Jack broaches the idea of selling the farm, why the sudden family interest after all these years?'

Erin stared. The dark eyes were challenging hers—and she could see clearly what was behind the question.

Somehow she made herself speak. It took more strength than she knew she possessed.

'I guess...I guess I see what you're thinking,' Erin managed finally, her voice trembling. She walked forward and placed her hands on the table, her eyes huge in her white face. 'You think I've been sent over to get what I can for us. Is that what you think?'

'It's the obvious conclusion,' Mike agreed calmly.
'The local land agent told me Jack was thinking of selling because he knew I'd be interested in buying if the
farm is sold. Then suddenly we have family interest. A
lonely old man suddenly has family after twenty long
years.'

'A lonely old man suddenly has me,' Erin whispered.

Erin could hardly think. Her mind was a kaleidoscope
of impressions—and the overriding feeling was pain.
This man was judging people she loved. Judging her
father…

All these years the locals here had been thinking her
father was a heartless, uncaring emigrant.

She wondered vaguely if her father knew what was
thought of him in the place he still regarded as home.
How it would hurt if he guessed! Her father loved this
place more than she did.

'Erin…' Mike rose from his chair. The colour had
bleached completely from Erin's face and he could see
the pain washing through her eyes. He'd be a fool if he
couldn't see it—and if there was one thing Mike
McTavish wasn't it was a fool.

He moved swiftly behind her and his hands dropped
to her shoulders. 'Erin, don't look like that. You can't
help what your father is.'

The touch of his hands burned through the light fabric
of Erin's shirt. She wanted comfort so much. She wanted
this man's arms around her so much it was a physical
ache. Yet here he was hurting her—hurting those she
loved. What she felt in her heart was so far from common sense that Erin felt herself almost torn in two. She
pulled away in real distress.

'Don't you touch me,' she whispered. 'Don't…'

'I only…'

'You only thought you'd comfort me,' she managed,
and then caught herself. Comfort her? Mike McTavish
had done that once before and ten years of heartache had

ensued. Well, she wasn't taking any comfort from him
now.

'I don't need your comfort,' she said bleakly. 'I don't
need anything you have on offer, Mike McTavish, and
my father sure as heck doesn't need your good opinion.
My father was brought up next door to you—he's told
me he and your father were good friends—and yet after
we arrived in Pittsburgh all my father's letters to yours
went unanswered. He wondered why. And now I know.
It was vicious, idle gossip and judgement. Judging things
you know nothing about. Well, you and all the people
in this nosy, judgemental district can take a long hike
for all I care. There's only my grandfather that matters.'

And, to her horror, she felt tears welling up and threatening to fall.

Erin blinked—and blinked again. And then she
sniffed.

She was darned if she was going to cry before this
man. No way!

She didn't cry. She never cried!

She wiped the threatening tears angrily away with one
hand while fending off Mike McTavish's comfort with
the other. A hand went down to her jeans pocket, searching for a tissue—and found nothing.

'Don't touch me,' she whispered again.

'I won't.'

Mike had seen the searching hand, though. Without
comment, he handed her a large, man's handkerchief and
then stood back watching—as one would watch a
strange, unknown creature one didn't know how the
heck to deal with.

Erin accepted the handkerchief with real gratitude.
She blew her nose hard and glared—and, to her disgust,
found Mike McTavish was smiling.

'A good blow always makes you feel better.' Then,
as Erin looked helplessly down at the handkerchief, his
grin deepened.

'You seem to accuse me of being landed gentry,' he

smiled. 'Well, here's a gesture for you. Keep the hand-kerchief. I can afford it!'

'Th—thanks,' she whispered, her anger disappearing and an awful grimness seeping in. She'd exposed herself with this man—and she didn't like it one bit.

As always, when feeling her worst, Erin sought for laughter. She looked down at the damp handkerchief.

'Are you sure you want me to keep it?' she managed. 'There's three perfectly good quarters left.'

'I'm absolutely sure.' Mike's smile was one of pure admiration.

Erin's watery smile faded. If only he didn't make her feel so…so… So like being fourteen years old all over again!

'I'm…I'm going home now,' she whispered. 'Tell the twins…tell the twins they're welcome to visit me. If they cut across the paddocks it's a safe walk to my grandpa's farm—but I won't be coming back here.'

Mike nodded, as if her statement had been expected. 'I'll tell them.'

'You will let them come?' Erin found herself suddenly anxious. 'You will let them visit?'

'The twins can visit whoever they like,' Mike said calmly. 'And I'm sure they'd love to see you again.'

Implying that Mike McTavish wouldn't, Erin thought bleakly. Erin could hear that decision clearly in his voice.

'Fine.' Erin practised her glare one last time, even if her glare was still watery. Mike's dark eyes were watching her calmly now, unsmiling. 'I'll go…'

She turned to the door but the door was flung open before she reached it.

'Mike…Erin, come quick…' It was Laura, white faced with terror, bursting through the door and almost falling with the force of her entry. 'Erin, Matthew's on Paddy and Paddy took off down the paddock so fast I can't catch him. And he's taking Matthew away…'

CHAPTER FOUR

PADDY and Matthew were well away.

Mike and Erin burst through the back door as one—to find the yard empty. Paddy had been hitched to the trough. There was no Paddy and no Matthew.

'Where…?' Mike gazed round, fast. There was no sign of boy or horse.

'Paddy wanted something to eat,' Laura faltered. 'At least, we thought he did. So me and Matt took him over into the wheat paddock—just to give him a taste…'

'The wheat paddock…' Mike was already starting to run, his big hand gripping Laura's. Erin ran too, unsure of where they were going but darned if she was being left behind. 'Laura, you did say Matt was on the horse?' Mike demanded. They were halfway across the yard, Laura being half carried by the speed of Mike's run.

'Matt wanted to get up on Paddy's back,' Laura sobbed, breathless from running. 'So we held Paddy near the gate and Matt climbed on. And Matt said "Giddyup" and Paddy did. They rode all the way up the paddock and Paddy was going really, really fast and Matt yelled "stop" but Paddy didn't…'

Neither did Mike. He ditched Laura's hand and his long legs left both Erin and Laura behind. By the time Erin reached the gate behind the house, Mike was already through, shading his eyes and trying desperately to see across the sea of wheat.

The wheat paddock was immense. There must be half a mile of rolling wheat almost ready for harvest, Erin guessed, shading her own eyes to see up the distant hills.

And there they were—horse and boy—still magically together. Paddy was galloping up the far slope, his mane flying in the breeze as he cut a swathe through the wheat, with Matt clinging on for dear life.

'Matt…' Laura screamed and Mike's hand gripped down hard on the little girl's shoulder.

'I'll never reach them…' Mike's face was taut with fear, his face riveted to horse and boy. 'He'll come off. Dear God… Stay here with Erin, Laura, and I'll get the farm bike.' He wheeled to run back to the shed, but Erin's hand came out and caught him by the wrist.

'Wait.'

'But…' He tried to shake her off but Erin clung hard. 'He'll be killed…'

'He's sitting well. Watch him,' Erin said urgently. Erin's eyes were tuned to the pair now, watching them move as one. Matt was in no danger of falling, as long as Paddy didn't find a rabbit hole.

'Erin, let me go…'

Erin wasn't listening. As Mike hauled his wrist from her grasp she released it almost casually. Calmly she lifted her two index fingers to her mouth, put them firmly between her teeth—and blew.

Her whistle would have woken the dead. The two farm dogs who were Mike's constant shadows leaped about a foot and then whined and slunk behind Mike's heels.

The whistle carried as nothing else could.

From half a mile away, Paddy's head turned. He slowed as he sought the source of the whistle.

And then the big horse saw the distant speck that was his mistress—and he headed for home.

Still he was galloping. He was travelling too fast over unknown ground, Erin thought swiftly, and she cupped her hands and yelled.

'Whoa, Paddy. Whoa, boy…'

The horse slowed again and stopped, confused.

Then another short whistle.

And Paddy started to move again, but this time at a gentle canter. He came slowly towards them through the waist-high wheat, bearing his child rider as if carrying nothing at all.

Beside Erin, Mike and Laura were motionless, each riveted by what they were seeing. They seemed almost afraid to break the silence.

Finally the big, old horse reached his mistress. Paddy came straight to Erin's side, halted hard against her and blew into her hair.

Aren't I clever? he seemed to be saying. I did just what you told me.

Erin hugged the lean, velvety nose and then looked up at Matt.

And Matthew was beaming like all his Christmases had come at once.

'Did you see us go?' the little boy whispered, so excited his tongue tripped over the words. He leaned down and patted Paddy's neck without a trace of fear. 'Did you see us gallop? I didn't fall off once, and Paddy's the most beautiful horse I've ever seen in my life. Did he come because you whistled, Erin?'

Matt sat upright on the big horse's back, his legs much too short for the stirrups but his hands holding the reins loosely like a master.

'I couldn't make him stop by myself,' he admitted. 'I didn't know how, and…and I don't know how to whistle like that. Please, Erin, will you teach me?'

The child's small face was intensely serious and his voice was quivering with passion. Erin looked up at him and her face softened. Once, long ago, her father had flung her onto the back of a lovely horse—and she'd felt exactly the same.

She'd fallen off, though! There was inherent talent in this child. A gift.

'Of course I'll teach you.' She smiled. 'It will be entirely my pleasure.'

'Matt…'

The hoarse voice belonged to Mike. Mike McTavish was standing beside Erin as though struck dumb. Now he moved, stepping forward to reach up and lift his nephew down. 'You young…' Words failed him.

Mike held his nephew close and looked sternly into his face, but the shining intensity on the child's face stopped the reprimand in its tracks.

'I really rode him, Mike,' Matt whispered, his face a mix of wonder and pride. 'I really rode him.'

Erin had reached up and taken Paddy's reins from Matt. She stroked the horse's nose and smiled across at the little boy. This was a different child from the timid, fearful twin of yesterday.

And Mike… Her first impressions of Mike McTavish had been right. He couldn't be cruel to these children. He was just as kind and loving as she'd remembered for so long. As loving as she'd dreamed…

And for a fleeting second she found it in herself to be jealous of Matt. Of the child held so tightly against Mike's heart.

Stupid thought…

'He…he doesn't usually gallop off like that,' she told them all, slowly forcing her eyes away from Mike's. 'Matt, what did you do to make him move?' She fixed her features into mock severity. 'You didn't kick him, I hope.'

'Of course I didn't.' Matt was wounded to the core by such a suggestion. 'I just leaned over and told him to go. I said, "Giddyup. Go, Paddy, Go" and just touched his sides with my feet and then we were flying…'

And Matt was still flying.

'Well, if you intend to gallop on a horse as big as Paddy, you'd better come over to our farm tomorrow and have a proper lesson, Matt McTavish,' Erin said, smiling. 'Let's teach you how to walk sedately before you go scaring the pants off your uncle and me.'

'You'll teach me?'

'Of course I'll teach you,' Erin said promptly.

'The children already have lessons—' Mike told her, but was cut off short by Matthew.

'Not proper lessons,' the little boy breathed. 'Aunt Caroline takes us back to her place. She sends us down to Mr Higgs and he puts us on the back of two ponies who are so fat they don't even want to walk.'

'He's taught you at least to have light hands,' Erin smiled, looking doubtfully at Mike.

'Mr Higgs didn't teach me that,' Matt said scornfully. 'I watch horses whenever they're on TV.'

'But if Mr Higgs is already teaching you…'

'He doesn't teach us. He just makes the ponies go round and round the yard while he gets on with his work and every now and then he yells at us.'

'Well…' Erin shrugged. She smiled up at Mike. 'Mike, I'm happy to teach them.'

'Me too?' Laura asked breathlessly. Then she looked doubtfully up at Paddy. 'But Paddy's awfully big. I don't like Aunt Caroline's ponies much, but…'

'My grandfather has a very gentle and pretty grey mare who might do you nicely.' Erin smiled. 'Grandpa rides a rather magnificent black stallion called Blaze and I think he keeps Tessa to keep Blaze company.'

'Your grandfather still rides?' Mike asked incredulously, and Erin nodded.

'Yes.' The day Jack O'Connell stopped riding would be the day they buried him, Erin thought affectionately, remembering the way Jack had introduced Paddy to his new stablemates the night before.

'I haven't seen him on a horse for months.' Mike's tone suggested Erin didn't know what she was talking about and Erin flushed.

'Maybe he doesn't come this way much any more.'

'But he still rides?'

'Absolutely.'

'Then why doesn't he come near here?' Mike said slowly. 'I don't understand.'

'I do,' Erin told him flatly. 'Grandpa tells me he last

rode this way three months ago—and Caroline saw him
taking a jump over hedges on the bottom boundary.
Caroline told him politely that trespassers would be
prosecuted—so he hasn't been back.'

'That's ridiculous.' Mike's face was growing thunderous.

'I must be making it up,' Erin agreed politely, and
then smiled. 'We members of the lower echelons are
known for make-believe.' She watched him sympatheti-
cally as his face stiffened to rigid fury. There were things
Mike McTavish didn't understand about his precious
Caroline and it wasn't Erin's place to inform him—but
it didn't hurt to drop a few hints.

'Look, if Caroline did that then she mustn't have realized who he was.'

'Of course not,' Erin agreed, pretending to ignore his
fury. 'Now…will you let me teach the twins?'

'Look… Miss O'Connell…'

'I'm quite happy with you calling me Erin.' Erin
placed a foot in Paddy's stirrup and swung herself lightly
up onto Paddy's high back before calmly looking down
again at Mike. 'Yes, Mr McTavish?'

Mike practically ground his teeth. His fury was almost
tangible.

'If I have to call you Erin then you call me Mike,' he
snapped. 'And, Erin, it's all very well you offering to
teach the twins to ride…'

'I'm not doing that.' Erin smiled sweetly. 'If Matt can
ride Paddy like he did today I can't say I'll teach him
to ride.' Her mischievous smile encompassed Matt.
'Matthew can already ride. All I'll be doing is teaching
him the finer points—like how to stop.'

'Will you let me get a word in edgeways?' Mike was
practically speechless with rage.

'Sir!'

He glared. Silence.

'You wished to say something?' Erin prodded politely. 'I'm being quiet—sir.'

It was too much for the twins. They broke into giggles, fought to control them—and then peeped cautiously at their uncle.

Mike wasn't smiling. He looked like a man at the end of his rope.

'Erin O'Connell, thank you for the offer of lessons,' he growled at last. 'But we don't want them.'

This time the silence was different. The laughter died completely from the twins' faces and Erin frowned.

'Why not?'

'Because the twins have been having lessons with Caroline's groom for two months and I want them to have some continuity.'

'Meaning?' Erin's face grew still.

'Meaning you'll be gone again soon.'

Erin's eyes flashed. 'Define "soon".'

'Look, I have no idea of how long you're staying, but I assume the farm will be being sold and you'll be off again—'

'Taking my pound of flesh with me.'

'I didn't say that.'

'It's what you implied,' Erin said coolly. 'That I'm here for my share of my grandfather's farm. And I don't like the implication.'

'But you are just here for a holiday?' Mike demanded, his eyes meeting hers. Challenging.

'As a matter of fact I'm not,' Erin said slowly. 'Do you think I'd go to all the trouble of quarantining Paddy if I were just here for a few weeks?'

'Paddy's an American horse?' Mike asked incredulously, and Erin nodded.

'That's right. Straight from the land of stars and stripes.' She managed to smile, reaching down to rub Paddy's long neck. 'And here to hobnob with the colonials down under—in between keeping his very own tramp owner happy, of course.'

'So...how long do you intend staying?'

'I'm here for as long as my grandfather will have me,'

she said softly. Erin took a deep breath and met Mike's look. Unconsciously her chin tilted in defiance. 'So...I may live to be a thorn in your side for a very long time.'

'You're staying for ever?' Laura asked breathlessly, and Erin looked down at her and smiled.

'Yes,' she said simply. She looked back at Mike. 'So... I can teach the children riding if that's what they'd like.'

'Mike, please...please...' It was Matthew, clinging to his uncle and his face alive with passion. 'Please, Uncle Mike. You have to let us. Please...'

'I'll speak to Caroline about it.'

'But she won't let us. I know she won't. She won't let us and she doesn't matter. It's you who decides. Please, Uncle Mike.'

Mike's face closed.

'Caroline does matter,' he told his nephew briefly. He looked up at the girl on the horse with the same stern look.

'Thank you for your offer, Miss O'Connell,' he told her. 'I'll let you know.'

Erin stared at him for one long moment, and then nodded. As a dismissal it was absolute.

Without another word she touched Paddy's flanks— and Erin O'Connell and her horse took themselves home.

CHAPTER FIVE

MIKE let her know that night.

Jack retired early, sticking to the habits of an old man used to living by himself. Erin cleaned the farmhouse kitchen and then wandered out to the verandah. Sadie, Grandpa's fat labrador, greeted Erin with sedate dignity, and together they settled to watch the stars emerge in the night sky.

The constellation of stars making the Southern Cross was just where Erin had left it ten years ago, hanging low in the southern sky.

Erin nestled into Grandpa's rocker and it felt like home.

Except things weren't right.

This was supposed to be a time of calm, necessary to soothe Erin's jumpy nerves, but the episode with Mike McTavish in the afternoon had unsettled her completely. Mike McTavish had disturbed her too much to allow her nerves to still.

She couldn't be restful. The evening was soft and balmy. The noises of the farm had died away, leaving only the absolute hush that was to be found on farmland far from town.

It was the silence Erin had come half a world to find, and yet now she had it she couldn't enjoy it. And when the old dog bristled beside her and lumbered over to stare down the steps into the night, Erin knew who was coming even before Mike's tall shape emerged from the gloom.

'Miss O'Connell?'

Sadie gave a half-hearted bark but the dog must have

recognized the newcomer. Mike McTavish must have been here before.

'What…what do you want?' Erin whispered.

As a welcome it was ungracious to say the least, but it was all Erin was capable of. She didn't rise. Grandpa's rocker stilled, but Erin's body felt strangely listless. She was reluctant to rise and greet this man. It was almost as if she was afraid of him.

'I came to talk to you about riding lessons.'

Erin gave her chair a gentle rock. 'You have Aunt Caroline's permission, then?' she asked.

Mike's breath drew in sharply. He leapt lightly up onto the verandah, scorning the steps used by lesser mortals, and stood looking down at Erin in the near dark.

The hall window was lit behind them, casting an eerie light over Erin's face, but Mike McTavish was in thick gloom.

'I don't ask Caroline's permission…' He glowered.

Erin winced. She felt darned uncomfortable where she was—like a prisoner being interrogated under a naked light with her captor out of sight. 'I'm sorry,' she said slowly. 'I shouldn't have said that.' She took a deep breath. 'I guess…I guess it's just that I didn't take to Caroline very much.'

There was a moment's silence. Mike shifted a bit, and suddenly Erin could see his face. It was thoughtful and grave.

'I guess that's fortunate,' he said at last. 'Because Caroline didn't take to you very much either.'

'Didn't she?' Despite her discomfort, Erin's irrepressible humour twinkled out. 'Now I wonder why that could be?'

'It couldn't be that you were rude to her?'

Erin pretended to consider.

'Nope,' she said at last. 'Caroline was rude to me before I gave her a hard time—so I guess her dislike was based on first impressions. My tramp image.'

'You criticized her.'

'So I did,' Erin agreed cordially. She wasn't fighting with Mike McTavish over whose fault it was. 'Well, that's sorted. What would you like me to do about it? Pistols at dawn?' She grinned into the dark. 'I should warn you, I'm a fair shot.'

'How about lunch on Sunday instead?'

Mike fixed her with what was meant to be a stern look, but Erin's twinkle caught him. The corners of his mouth twitched upward in response.

'That's not fair,' Erin said sadly. She shook her head. 'I want pistols. Caroline will win every time at Sunday lunch. Jack says she's cordon bleu trained and I'm the world's most hopeless cook.'

'You can't be worse than me.' Mike's body seemed to relax. He hauled up a wicker chair close to Erin's rocker and sank his long frame into it, turning towards Erin. Now his face was as much in the light as hers.

'I bet I am,' Erin declared. The light was weirdly intimate. Mike was watching her with a smile playing at his eyes, and the smile was doing strange things to Erin's insides.

'You can't be,' he declared, grinning. 'Ask the twins. I have trouble with cornflakes.'

'Well, I've burnt holes in three kettles in the last twelve months,' Erin confessed dolefully. 'You can't get worse than burning hot water.'

'You're kidding.'

'Would I lie about anything so serious?' Erin chuckled. 'Mr McTavish, sausages have been known to grow legs and hike off in fear when they see me coming. If they suffer cooking by Erin, first they burst and then they turn black. My all-time low was when I exploded a can of beans. I heated it first and then tried opening it—and traces can be seen to this day on a certain ceiling in a Pittsburgh kitchen. After that my mom locked me out of the kitchen, and even the horses look sideways at the bran I give them.'

'You must have some domestic qualities.'

'Nope,' Erin said dolefully. 'I don't cook and I don't sew. I use quilts so I don't have to make my bed, and I clean my bath when it starts feeling furry. My grandpa tells me Caroline is going to make you a wonderful wife, Mr McTavish—and you're lucky you have her. I'm intending to make a good farmer—but I need a wife myself.'

Mike's laugh rang out into the night—a rich, gentle laugh that made Sadie wag her tail in appreciation.

Even dogs were fair smitten by Mike McTavish.

What it did to Erin was worse. She didn't have a tail to wag—but she sure felt as if something was happening inside when this man laughed.

'Surely you're joking, though?' he smiled. 'I thought all women were domestic at heart?'

Erin's eyebrows hit her hairline. 'Yeah?' She grinned. 'You sound like a boy I went out with once who asked me to marry him—and almost in the same breath told me he was aching for someone to do his ironing. ''All women like ironing,'' he told me. He reckons it's bred into the genes. According to him, we have a little ironing board stamped into the far left corner of our brains at conception.'

'And your stamp missed the mark?'

'It sure did,' Erin chuckled. 'It might have landed on my left foot instead—so whenever I feel the urge to iron I firmly stomp on it.'

'I guess it's lucky I'm marrying Caroline, then.' Mike grinned, though the smile in his eyes held a hint of uncertainty. His eyes were watching Erin as though he couldn't make her out. She certainly wasn't the kind of woman he was accustomed to being near. 'I hate to tell you this, Miss O'Connell, but we wouldn't suit.'

'We certainly wouldn't,' Erin agreed, and to her fury she heard a faint note of desolation creep into her voice. She bit her lip hard and changed the subject. 'You…you want me to give the children riding lessons?'

'The children would love to have you give them riding lessons.'

Erin flushed. The correction in Mike's words was transparent.

'So…you don't really wish it but you're giving in to the children's pleading.'

'That's not what I said.'

'It's what you implied.'

'You read too much into what I say.'

'Okay…' Erin nodded. 'If you had your druthers, Mike McTavish, who would you have teach the children? Me? Or the unknown but despised Mr Higgs?'

'There's nothing wrong with Mr Higgs.'

'Then let him keep on teaching the twins,' Erin snapped. 'I'm not asking to teach the twins as a favour.'

'No. But the twins—'

'Will be unhappy.' Erin's face softened as she finished his sentence for him. For all this man's macho exterior and horrible misconceptions concerning the female of the species, Mike McTavish cared deeply for his brother's children. 'I know that,' she told him. 'And I don't think it will hurt to let me teach them.' She smiled. 'I am good…'

'I'm sure you are.'

There was just enough condescension in Mike's voice to make Erin flush. She bit her lip, temper rising—and then rose with decision.

'Stay where you are,' she ordered, and whisked herself inside.

It only took a moment to find what she was looking for. Apart from her riding gear, Erin's worldly possessions fitted into two suitcases. She'd brought nothing that wasn't useful—except for this: the small box that nestled in her hand as she hurried back to the verandah. Half of her was telling herself not to be stupid—that Mike would think she was showing off—and the other half was telling her this was a way of convincing him she could teach the twins.

Mike was still sitting where she had left him, lounging back and looking out at the night sky. He stirred as she reappeared and looked down curiously at what she held in her hand.

'What the…?'

Erin placed the box in his hands and Mike's voice died.

The medal was distinct. There was no mistaking it, even in the dim light, and this man had been around horses and horsey people enough to know what it meant.

Mike lifted the silver disc from its box with something close to reverence and then gazed up at her.

'The last Olympics?' There was awe in his voice.

'Yes,' Erin said softly. 'My skills haven't slipped all that much since then.'

'Silver… For dressage…'

'Paddy deserved gold,' she said apologetically. 'I wasn't good enough on the day.' She grinned ruefully. 'Nerves,' she confessed. 'Paddy would have done it. He was as good as the best. Better. I let him down.'

'Paddy!'

'Paddy's quite a horse.' She smiled. 'He's the best horse I've ever had by a country mile. I bought him cheap because he was such a failure as a steeplechaser— and he's just…just wonderful.'

'But…'

'But what?'

Mike hadn't risen from his chair. He was turning the medal over and over in his hands as if he couldn't believe it.

'You're not serious,' he said at last. 'If you're as good as this… Why on earth aren't you still at home—training for the next Olympics?'

'Paddy's too old,' Erin said softly. 'Too old to be travelling and going through quarantine all the time and taking the stress of international competition. I've promised him this is the last time he goes on a plane. And he's irreplaceable. It was Paddy who won that medal—not me.'

'But...' He shook his head. 'You're young. There are other horses to train.'

'None like Paddy. Anyway...'

'Anyway?'

'My grandfather needs me,' Erin said softly. 'How can I keep competing knowing Grandpa's here by himself? Or living in some unit because he's sold the farm.'

'You haven't given this up because of your grandfather?'

'What better reason?' Erin said lightly, and only she knew what soul-searching had gone into her decision.

Mike shook his head. He fingered the silver disc, and by the look on his face Erin knew he acknowledged the work and commitment behind this. What she'd sacrificed...

'You're an American citizen,' Mike said slowly. 'You must be to have competed...'

'Yes.'

'Then you can't compete for Australia unless you change citizenship. And that could take years.'

'I told you,' Erin said softly, shoving back the heartache the decision to retire had cost her. 'Paddy won that medal—and Paddy and I have retired.'

'Absolutely?'

'Absolutely.' There was no hint of uncertainty in Erin's voice. Her future was this farm. It was no longer in riding.

'You did this for your grandfather?' Mike said slowly, turning the medal over and over in his hands. 'You gave this up...?'

'No,' Erin said uncomfortably. 'I've had a lot of fun. I've been lucky. Now...this might be fun, too. Managing this farm. Taking care of Grandpa. I've just moved on...'

'But...' Mike shook his head as though clearing a fog. 'You'll teach Matthew and Laura?'

'I want to do that.'

'Why?' Mike's face was still, watching hers.

'I think…I think because I like them both very much. And I feel sorry for them.' She smiled suddenly. 'And Matthew has the lightest pair of hands I've ever seen on a kid that age. The thought of teaching him excites me.'

'Not Laura?'

'I haven't seen Laura on a horse yet. But she has courage and I can tell instinctively that she's kind. I can teach her to be good.'

'Well…' Mike's breath was let out on a sigh. He was watching her as one might watch a caterpillar just metamorphosed into the splendour of a butterfly. He looked as if he couldn't believe what he was seeing. 'This certainly changes things,' he said simply. 'Of course I'd love you to teach them—and Caroline will be delighted as well when she knows.'

'But…' Erin reached over and lifted the medal from Mike's hands. Their fingers touched for a fleeting second and Erin flinched. 'I'd rather… If you don't mind, Mike…I'd rather you didn't tell anyone about this.'

'Not tell…?' Mike stared. 'That's crazy. I can't understand why the locals don't know anyway. I would have thought Jack would have boasted to the world about his clever granddaughter.'

'He doesn't talk much about his family,' Erin said shortly. 'He's learned not to over the years. And I'd rather…I'd rather just be me here.' She hesitated, trying to explain. 'The fuss was fun,' she said simply. 'And some people try to live off past glory for years. But I…I want to move on.' She smiled. 'Don't get me wrong. I'm not being noble, here. I'll tell my grandkids if I ever have any. But for now…now I'd rather not be reminded of it.'

'You will miss it,' Mike said, watching her still, and his eyes showed that he understood her sacrifice. His eyes were troubled.

'Yes.' She spread her hands. 'Of course I will. But this…this will make up for it.'

'Living with your grandfather?'

'Yes.' She hesitated. 'You don't know how bad we've felt about him—all these years. You don't know how much we've worried about him—and how much pain my father's suffered knowing Grandpa was by himself. This is such a small thing. This—my decision—feels right for me. It's right for my grandfather and it's right for my father. Olympic glory seems a bit shallow in comparison.'

'I guess,' Mike said slowly, staring at her. He shook his head. 'No, Erin,' he said at last. 'I don't understand. I don't understand at all. Tell me about your father.'

'About…'

Mike leaned over and took her hand in his—strong and warm and compelling.

'Tell me why you're making the sacrifices your father should have made,' he told her.

CHAPTER SIX

SILENCE.

Erin stared out into the dark, her father's face before her. 'The sacrifices your father should have made' Mike had said. If only he knew.

This man, if any, should know. For some reason it was unbearable that Mike McTavish could judge her father harshly.

She stared down at their linked hands for a long moment. It seemed so right—the joining—and yet it was just an empty gesture of comfort.

And finally she found the strength to pull her hand away. She rose unsteadily to her feet and walked across to the edge of the verandah, staring out to the night sky.

Mike watched silently from his chair. He stayed where he was, sensing her need for space.

For a long moment—two or three minutes—Erin stayed silent, and there was an air of desolation about her that made Mike rethink his decision to let her be.

Finally he rose and crossed to stand beside her.

'Erin… Please…I'd like you to tell me why your father left here.'

He saw her flinch—and mistook the reason.

'I'm sorry,' he said quietly, taking a step back. 'I didn't mean to pry.'

'You didn't—you weren't…'

How to explain that it was the gentleness in Mike's tone that made Erin cringe? She'd longed for tenderness from this man for so long it was like a distant, all-pervasive dream.

Nonsense, of course. A nonsense dream.

She hesitated, not turning to Mike but still staring out

over the paddocks. It was as if she was speaking to the distant moonlit horizon.

She had to tell him. It was as if she was compelled. She couldn't bear that this man condemned the father she loved.

'My father has emphysema,' she said at last.

'Emphysema…'

'That's what I said,' Erin told him grimly. 'That's why he's been condemned by this community for so long. He was born with a condition called bullous emphysema. Dreadful crime…'

'Erin…'

'It's true, isn't it?' Erin flashed, wheeling to face Mike in the dark. 'My father, Richard O'Connell, abandoning his father and taking off to America without a backward glance. And, as far as this place goes, all Dad's reasons were selfish. How dare he leave his father alone to face old age without a family? That's what everyone said, isn't it?'

'Yes,' Mike said softly. 'But only because we didn't know better.' He reached out and gripped Erin's hands in his—and held her hard. 'Erin, forget the anger for a moment. Tell me about your father's illness.'

'We don't talk about it.'

'I know you don't talk about it,' Mike said grimly. 'Like you don't talk about Olympic medals. But maybe, just maybe you should be talking about this.'

'Why? It's none of your business.'

'No. And your grandfather's happiness is none of my business. But I've worried about him over the years and felt for his loneliness, so maybe I have been judgemental. Erin, tell me about your father.'

Erin stared down at their linked hands. She tried to pull back, but the hands held—strong and firm and unrelenting.

There seemed no choice but to tell.

'My Dad had childhood asthma,' she whispered finally, speaking to their linked hands. 'It was mild, but it concealed a worse problem. My Dad was born with bullous emphysema.'

Mike frowned. 'Bullous… Erin, I don't know what that is.'

'Hardly anyone does.' Erin hesitated, searching for words. 'I guess…' she said slowly, 'I guess the easiest way of explaining is by comparing lungs to a sponge. That's sort of what lungs look like under a microscope— thousands of tiny cells like a giant honeycomb. Only, in Dad's lungs, some of those cells are too big. The en- larged cells are called bullae, and they're always at risk of bursting. When they do, they let air into the chest wall and Dad can't breathe. He has to have emergency surgery or he dies.'

'But…' Mike looked as if he was struggling to un- derstand. 'Your dad had this from birth?'

'He did, but no one knew,' Erin said sadly. 'He says he was often breathless, but everyone put the breath- lessness down to his asthma.'

'So he's always been at risk of sudden death?'

'Yes. The doctors say he was lucky that none burst when he was small.' Erin looked up at Mike's face— and then quickly looked down again. There was sym- pathy and horror in Mike's eyes—and she couldn't deal with sympathy and horror from this man. Somehow she kept her voice working. 'Mike, you know my mom's American? When…when I was five Mom and Dad and I flew to the States to visit Mom's parents—and the change of pressure on the plane caused the first bulla to burst. Dad nearly died.'

'I don't believe this,' Mike said grimly. 'Why did we never know?'

Erin shrugged. 'Grandpa knew, of course—but maybe he was so upset he couldn't tell anyone. And afterwards Dad said he didn't want people knowing. You see, we were stuck. Absolutely. Dad had all sorts of tests. He'd lost more of his lung capacity, so his breathlessness was worse, and he was told he mustn't do hard physical work. He was told he couldn't fly again—not even to fly home—and he was told he must always be near a major operative hospital in case there were further problems. He's had three bullae burst so far—and each time has been frightening—but in between he's built a fairly normal life.'

Mike's face was frankly stunned. 'My father didn't know this. And he and your father were friends.'

'Dad didn't want sympathy,' Erin explained. 'He hated people knowing. He still does. So, he and Grandpa agreed. Dad couldn't work the farm, even if he could get back here. So they told everyone we were staying in America—and we got on with our lives.' She smiled 'Dad's had a good life, really, even though he's missed the farm so much. He's had fun. He found a job as an agent for an Australian stock and station firm in Pittsburgh, so he sold farms from a desk in the city. He even enjoys it. And me...' She shrugged. 'I ached for farms. Horses were in my blood—but luckily my maternal grandparents had a small farm just out of town. I was there nearly every weekend.'

'But...your Dad's okay?'

'He's had a couple of bad episodes,' Erin told him. 'But he's good now—cheerful even. Until Grandpa's letter came, saying he was selling the farm.'

'And then?'

'Dad can't come back,' Erin said softly. 'We all know that. So, we had a round-table conference and decided I'd come instead.'

'I...I see.' Mike's voice was expressionless. 'So you've come half a world because your grandpa needs you.'

'Yes.'

'And your father misses out now again. He misses out on you.'

'I guess he does.' Erin's face clouded. 'My parents and I are very close...but so are we to Grandpa. And this way there's two members of our family in each place instead of three in America and one here.'

'Couldn't your dad come out here by ship—at least for a visit? Maybe with private nursing?' Mike said slowly.

Erin sighed. 'No. Don't think we haven't considered it. But it wouldn't just be private nursing. He'd need his own surgeon, for heaven's sake. Imagine how much that would cost! An absolute fortune, I'd imagine—which we don't possess.'

Mike shook his head. 'But it must have cost a fortune to put you through the Olympics—and then pack you up and ship Paddy over.'

'No.' Erin smiled, shaking sadness aside. 'I have a maternal uncle who thought my Olympic preparation was a great investment for his brag meter.'

'Brag meter?' Mike said faintly.

'Brag meter. He boasts about me ad nauseam to all his business acquaintances and, seeing he's a horse broker, he reckons my medal's done his credentials no end of good.' She smiled. 'He's great, and he's also great for finding me sponsors. And as for getting me and Paddy here—I got me a deal.' She grinned. 'A ripper.'

'A deal…' Mike released Erin's hands and stared. The transformations this elfin girl before him seemed capable of were amazing. There was no self-pity at all in the shy smile playing over her face, despite the story she'd just told him.

'Tell me about your deal, Erin,' he said faintly.

'A friend was bringing a string of stud racing stock over.' Erin smiled up at him. 'The strapper he usually employed wouldn't come because his wife was expecting a baby—so I worked my way over by taking his place. I earned my fare, Paddy's fare and quarantine expenses by caring for all my friend's horses while they were confined. Plus Paddy.' She smiled. 'That's why I was so disgusting when you first met me. All the horses were released from quarantine together and the deal was that I work until then. I cleaned out ten horses' quarters before bringing Paddy here.'

'I—I see.' Mike clearly didn't. He was staring at Erin in the dim light as if he couldn't believe his eyes. 'And—and now what?'

'And now Paddy and Grandpa and I are intending to live happily ever after,' Erin sighed. 'That's the plan.'

'You mean…live on this farm for always?'

'Yep.'

'What on earth do you know about farming?'

'I know a bit.' Erin bristled.

'Yeah?'

'Yeah.' Erin dug her hands in her jeans pockets and glared. 'I do, as a matter of fact. In between junketing round the world on horses I've squeezed in a couple of years of agricultural training.'

'I see.' Mike's weathered face creased into laughter. 'Agriculture American style.'

'Excuse me…?'

'Well, what did you learn, Miss Clever-Boots? How to grow maize on the prairies? How to round up buffalo herds?'

'You sound about eighty,' Erin said accusingly, and tilted her chin at him. 'More bigoted than my grandpa and that's saying heaps. I've convinced him I can try so you can just butt out, Mike McTavish. I know heaps. I've read and read…'

'Book learning!'

'And Grandpa knows it all and he can teach me…'

'Do you know how strapped for money this farm is?'

The question brought Erin up hard. The conversation to now had been all light-hearted banter—and suddenly it wasn't.

'Yes,' she said slowly. Her hands were on her denim-clad hips and she took a step back, deliberately putting her face into shadow. 'I know. Do you?'

'I know your grandpa's in trouble.'

'Along with the whole district, I'll bet,' Erin said bitterly. She stared up at him. 'Grandpa says you're interested in buying.'

'That's right.'

'Is that why you're so interested in what I'm doing?'

Mike sighed. 'No, it's not. Do you have to be so darned touchy?'

'It's not being touchy to protect my grandpa from—'

'From wealthy landgrabbers,' Mike said sardonically. 'Is that what you think I am?'

'I'm not sure what you are,' Erin said softly. She winced inside. She did know. Mike McTavish was dangerous to her, whether he was threatening to buy her grandpa's farm or not. He was dangerous because of the way he made her feel.

Her face clouded in the moonlight and Mike saw her uncertainty. 'Hey, Erin,' he said gently. 'You must know I can't buy your grandpa's farm without his consent. It's just... You can't live next door to a farm without realizing the place hasn't been making much of an income for the past few years, and things are going backward.'

'I can see that.' Erin's voice was strained. It seemed wrong to be discussing Grandpa's financial situation with this stranger.

He wasn't a stranger, though. He was Mike McTavish.

'So what are you going to do about it?' Mike asked.

'Fix it.'

He grinned then. 'I know that, Wonder Woman,' he teased gently. 'But let's look at the short term. Like the coming winter. How much feed do you have?'

'I'll just bet you know,' Erin said bitterly. 'We have some silage but no hay.'

'There's heaps of hay just waiting to be harvested in your bottom paddocks. There's been no stock in there for months.'

'I know that.'

'Well?'

Erin grimaced. 'I don't think—'

'You can't afford a team to do the harvesting?'

'No, we can't,' Erin said bluntly. 'We need new equipment and we can't afford it. I'll get a bit in myself, but, for the main, we've decided to hope for a mild winter. If we don't get it then we'll sell stock off.'

'I have a better idea.'

'Which is?'

'Let me send my men over and bring the hay in for you.'

Silence.

Erin bit her lip.

'I don't… I don't think…'

'You don't think your grandpa will agree?' Mike said softly. 'I'm damned sure he won't. And the reason I know is that I've already offered. Did he tell you of my offer before you started throwing accusations that I was only after his land?'

'No.'

'Well, it's true.' Mike shrugged. 'Though what your grandpa said to me was pretty much the same accusation. He said I could take control here when he finally sold— and not before.' Mike's face softened as Erin's face fell in dismay and he put a finger up to touch her face.

It was a brief gesture of comfort—nothing more—and it was like a caress.

'Don't look like that, Erin,' Mike said softly. 'There's no need. Your grandpa is a crusty old man but I understand him well enough. He's so scared of losing control. He's so scared of losing this place. If you've indeed come home to stay then you've given him a very great gift—and I intend to give you all the support I can.'

It was too much. Erin put her hand up and brushed away Mike's fingers from her face, feeling the hot sting of tears behind her eyes. She turned away.

'I don't—I can't…'

'Why don't you?' Mike asked calmly. 'And why can't you?'

'Look, Mr McTavish…'

'Mike.'

'Mike.' She turned back to him, her face desperate. 'It's very—it's very kind of you. But my grandpa won't agree.'

'He will if you pay.'

Erin moistened her dry lips with the tip of her tongue. She was right out of her depth here. She was out of her depth just standing on the verandah in the soft night light talking to this man.

'H—how?'

'You already have, in a sense.' Mike smiled. 'You rescued my niece and nephew—'

'I told Caroline…' Erin interrupted savagely. 'Neighbours don't accept payment for bringing each other's kids home.'

'No. But they do accept that their neighbours are grateful. And…' he smiled '…if you accept, also, that your services in teaching Matthew and Laura to ride are worth a heap to me… You have to accept that, and so will your Grandpa. How about twelve months' riding lessons for Matt and Laura in return for harvesting the hay, Miss O'Connell? Your lessons are worth much more than the cost of harvesting because of your qualifications, but, seeing I can't boast of your prowess, I've deducted a bit. The bargain seems fair, wouldn't you say? And it's renegotiable in twelve months when the hay's due for harvesting again.'

Erin stared.

The hay harvested… The haystacks filled. A full winter's feed for as many cattle as she liked—and, if she was lucky with the loaded paddocks, there might even be some hay left to sell.

She could convince Grandpa if she thought Mike was getting value for money. And she could give value.

'I—I…' She stammered the word at him and then bit her lip. 'It's very kind…'

'It's not kind at all,' Mike said firmly. He reached out and took her hand. 'It's business. Now, walk me back down to the boundary fence while we settle details. I have to get back. Dan, my foreman, is watching a movie in my kitchen and keeping an eye on the twins but I promised I'd be back in an hour.'

Erin stared down at their linked hands. 'I don't...'

Mike gave her hand a tug, grabbed the other and leapt lightly down from the verandah, propelling her down with him.

'Come on, Miss Erin O'Connell.' He laughed, steadying her with two strong hands as she landed. 'It's a lovely moonlit night and it's not too far to walk back alone from your boundary. Or...' He laughed down into her anxious face. 'Are you afraid of spectres and headless horsemen?'

'Not—not spectres.'

'Of me?' His smile deepened. 'I'm a happily engaged man, Miss O'Connell, with so many dependents I've lost count. Plus I have scores of my ancestors buried within disapproval distance of this place. I do something they don't like and I feel their combined condemning weight sitting square on my shoulders.' He smiled. 'So...I'll walk you to the fence, Miss O'Connell, but I'll be a picture of propriety. Much as I'd like not to be.'

Erin stared up at him.

'You don't...' They were already walking away from the house. Mike's hand was brooking no resistance as he pulled her forward. 'You don't mean that.'

Mike hesitated then. He walked a few more paces and then turned to face her. They were straight underneath one of the taller gums now, its vast canopy protecting them from the glimmer of starlight and its shadow making the night deep and dark.

'I guess I don't,' Mike said slowly. 'You're an attractive woman, though, Erin O'Connell. It's my guess you won't be staying with your grandpa for this lifetime you're talking of.'

'Now that...' Erin said slowly '...that is definitely none of your business.' She looked down at their linked hands, though she could hardly see them in the dark.

She could certainly feel them, though. 'Let me go, please, Mike,' she whispered. 'You…you have Caroline and I have…I have my grandpa.'

'So how are you going to get these grandkids to show your medal to, oh, independent Erin O'Connell?'

He was laughing at her, but there was a note of seriousness in his voice that undermined Erin's defences. It made her feel infinitely vulnerable.

'Maybe I'll borrow Laura and Matthew's children,' she said, trying to make her voice light. 'Then I'll have grandkids by proxy.'

'I reckon they'd be proud.' There was no missing the seriousness in Mike's voice now. There was also the husk of something that sounded suspiciously like the first stirrings of passion.

This was a man used to having his way with women. This was a man not yet accustomed to the confines of an engagement.

'Mike…let me go…' Erin tugged back, and to her relief she was released. 'I'm not—I'm not coming further with you. I don't think…'

'You don't think it'd be wise.' Mike nodded slowly. 'Maybe you're right. I have to keep reminding myself that the days of my bachelorhood are over.'

'I think that'd be sensible.' Erin took a step back, her voice crisp and breathless. Whoa, she told her racing heart.

She turned hard away.

'Are you coming to lunch on Sunday?'

Mike's demand halted Erin's retreat. She stood uncertainly, and slowly turned back.

'Sunday…'

'Caroline's asked a few people for a casual lunch,' Mike told her. 'We'd be pleased if you and Jack would come.'

'We… I'll have to ask Jack.'

'You do that,' Mike said softly. He stepped forward on the dry leaves and the sound of his one footstep cracking twigs was enough to make Erin draw in her breath and flinch.

The way she was feeling she half expected Mike McTavish to grasp her shoulders—and to draw her close.

She half wanted him to.

Mike did no such thing. Instead, Mike McTavish touched her again with that feathery touch of a caress. He placed one finger lightly against her pale cheek.

'The twins are counting on you coming,' he said softly. 'I'm counting on it. Don't let us down.'

Erin looked up at him with huge, frightened eyes. 'I…I won't…'

She took a step back—and Mike's hands did come out then, seizing her waist and dragging her forward.

'No… No…' It was a breathless whisper, half of indignation and half of entreaty.

'Hey, Erin.' Mike laughed down into her face then, his smile still beguiling in the dim light. 'I'm not intending rape here, Erin—or even a spot of no-good.'

'Then let me go.'

'Just let me move you.'

'No.' Erin shoved hard, hauling herself backwards. She took two steps back—and her boot squelched into one huge, fresh cow pat.

'You shouldn't have done that,' Mike said mournfully, his voice laced with laughter. 'I did try to stop you.'

'You…' Erin hauled her mired boot from the mess and glared. 'You…'

'I guess Sir Walter Raleigh would have thrown his coat down over the dung instead of grabbing his lady and hauling her sideways.' Mike sighed. 'Guess it's just as well you're not royalty. I might have had my head chopped off.'

'You still might if you keep laughing at me,' Erin snapped. 'I'm going inside.'

'For a bath?' Mike nodded. 'Very wise. From this angle, Erin O'Connell, I'd say you were a trifle on the

nose.' He grinned. 'See you Sunday, then? With or without cow dung.'

'I'll see you Sunday,' Erin said through gritted teeth,
and turned and stalked away with as much dignity as
she could muster.

It was a bit hard to muster dignity when she
squelched.

CHAPTER SEVEN

TO HER surprise, Jack O'Connell made no objection to the Sunday invitation.

'I won't go if you don't think we should,' Erin told her grandfather tentatively—and half hopefully—but Jack shook his head.

'If you're intending to stay here and live, you need some social life, girl,' he growled. 'You'll go crazy stuck here with me all the time. And I don't mind McTavish. It's that cold-faced cow he's got himself engaged to I find objectionable, and it'll be worth going just so she'll have to shake my hand and acknowledge me as a neighbour—instead of threatening me with the law if I trespass.'

'Mike said that was a mistake,' Erin said.

'Yeah?' Jack grimaced. 'Seems to me if anyone gets in that one's way she'll go for them with more than the law. It's a tough biddy he's got himself hooked by.'

'She's doing the best she can for the twins,' Erin said weakly, and then faltered. What on earth was she doing, defending a woman she disliked so much?

'Is she?' Jack threw back at her. 'What's in it for her, then? Marriage with the district's biggest landholder, that's what. She might even smile for that. She might be nice to anyone—even a couple of unwanted children—until the knot's tied.'

By the time Sunday rolled around Erin was distinctly nervous. 'Casual lunch', it seemed, might be more than that.

'Caroline's working and working,' the twins had informed her. The morning after Mike's visit they'd both appeared for their riding lesson, and by Saturday they were firm friends with Jack as well as Erin. 'The men have put a pretty white tent up on the lawn under the oak trees,' they'd told Erin. 'And there's three ladies cooking in the kitchen and someone's bringing in glasses and heaps and heaps of bottles...'

Oh, help, Erin thought, and consulted her wardrobe.

Her wardrobe didn't help one bit.

'With or without cow dung,' Mike had said, and by the look of her wardrobe that was just about all the choice she had. Every cent Erin had ever earned had gone into the costs of international competition. There was never anything for frivolity.

For 'frivolity', read one nice sophisticated little outfit that would make Erin look more than fourteen years old.

She just didn't have one—and there was no money to drive into Hamilton and buy such an outfit. Finally, Erin donned a dress her mother had made her three years ago. It was a simple, soft shirt-waister, eminently practical for weddings, funerals and equestrian functions where Erin's sole aim was to disappear into the crowd.

She doubted this dress would make her disappear in the lunch she was planning on attending. The dress was so simple it would probably make her stand out like a sore thumb.

Or an impoverished neighbour.

'Rats,' she told the mirror as she looked at her reflection.

The dress looked decidedly home-made, and ever so slightly shabby. A button had come off the front and Erin had sewn it back on herself with thread that didn't quite match. The soft green colour suited her and made her look pretty, but...

'It looks "Country Mouse",' she told her reflection.

At least she *was* a country mouse now, she thought, a bubble of happiness bursting through her depression. A farm mouse. On a farm which could be her home for life.

Her bubble of pleasure didn't make the outfit any more elegant. She grimaced at the odd thread on the offending button.

'What I need is to do what Mike McTavish's done,' she sighed. 'Find myself a nice suitable wife to keep me in order. A homemaker. It's not fair. I reckon I need Caroline almost as much as Mike McTavish.'

The thought of Caroline Podger reorganizing her life was enough to give Erin the giggles. She put her tongue out at her reflection, brushed her chestnut curls into something approaching submission and went to find Grandpa.

Jack was fighting his waistcoat.

'Dratted thing won't do up,' he said anxiously, looking up as his granddaughter knocked at his bedroom door. 'Eh, Erin, you do look pretty.'

'Pretty average,' Erin smiled. She slipped her hands into Jack's waistcoat and pulled it away from his shirt and off his shoulders. 'It's much too hot for a waistcoat,' she told him affectionately.

'Do you reckon?'

'I reckon.'

Jack swung to the mirror and eyed both their reflections with anxiety.

'We're not very grand, Erin lass.'

Erin pretended to consider.

'Nope,' she said at last. 'I guess we're not. They're just going to have to content themselves with our brilliant minds and our beautiful souls.'

Brilliant minds and beautiful souls weren't enough.

Erin reached the front gate of the McTavish place and quailed inwardly. Brilliant minds and beautiful souls obviously took second place here today. What took precedence was beautiful people.

This was a 'Who's Who' meet of the district, she decided in dismay, and she felt Jack stiffen beside her as he stared out at the well-dressed crowd of young couples scattered through the gardens.

They were driving Erin's truck—Jack's utility truck being even shabbier than Erin's. The truck looked absolutely incongruous among the Range Rovers and Bentleys parked along the drive.

'Can't we just slope off home now?' Jack said miserably, eyeing the offending vehicles. 'I thought this'd be a bunch of locals—but I don't know any of these cars. And I don't know any of these people.'

It was too late. The twins were lying in wait for them and swooped before Erin could even reply.

'Come on. Come on,' Laura announced, hauling Erin's door open and tugging her out of the truck. 'We've been waiting for you for ages because no one talks to us.'

The twins weren't the only ones waiting.

As Erin and Jack were propelled round the lawns to the magnificent white marquee Mike McTavish disassociated himself from a group of people in the garden and came to meet them.

He was casually dressed, but jeans had given way to tailored trousers and his open-necked shirt was good quality linen. With the soft wind blowing his hair and the sun in his eyes he looked altogether too good-looking for comfort!

For Erin's comfort...

Mike's smile was warm and all-encompassing as he strode across the lawn to meet them—and for a moment the combination of smile and man made Erin forget her dubious dress.

'Hi, Jack. Hi, Erin.' Mike took Jack's hand in a strong, warm clasp and smiled his heart-stopping smile down at Erin. 'I'm really pleased to see you both.'

And for a fraction of a second Erin thought she heard a faint echo of Laura's warmth and welcome in Mike's tone—as if he too felt out of place among these people.

It was imagination. Wishful thinking.

It had to be wishful thinking. This was none other than a good host playing his part. Mike was already offering Jack a beer, lifting a glass of champagne from a waiter's tray and pressing it into Erin's hands and calling his group of friends over to be introduced.

Mike McTavish was a smooth and practised host—nothing more—intent on making his guests welcome.

And then Caroline was by his side, smiling sweetly at Jack, her eyes flicking Erin with disdain—even as a wintry smile of welcome twisted her lips.

'I'm so pleased you could both come. It was a charming idea of Mike's to invite you.' Caroline laid a hand on Mike's arm, smiled possessively up at him and then directed her line of perfect teeth to Erin and Jack.

The twins swooped off. Where Caroline was, the twins weren't, Erin decided, and felt the same sort of wish herself.

Erin might come from Pittsburgh, but she certainly felt like the country mouse here today, she decided bitterly. Caroline looked stunning. Her tailored trousers and linen jacket must have cost almost as much as an economy airfare to America.

Or maybe a first-class airfare.

It was just as well Erin hadn't laid out good money on a new outfit. Anything she could have afforded would have looked 'Country Mouse' here today.

Come on, Erin, she told herself firmly. Get a grip on yourself. She was darned if she was being intimidated by the cost of someone's trousers!

'It was certainly kind of Mike to invite us.' Erin took a deep breath. 'I do want to get to know all the locals.'

She flashed Caroline her very best fund-raising smile and set about making the most of a bad afternoon.

And to a certain extent she enjoyed herself.

As a newcomer to the district, and an American, Erin was a novelty, and, as such, most of the people made an effort to meet her. They granted her one or two words, a quick assessment of her clothes and then they moved on. But Erin was doing a cursory summation of her own.

She was also eating.

The food was fabulous. There was no doubting Caroline's domestic ability, Erin decided as she helped herself from the groaning tables. There were exquisitely prepared hors d'oeuvres, three types of meat cooking slowly on three spits and as many as fifteen species of exotic salad.

The desserts were even better. Erin tucked into two helpings of black forest cake and Mike caught her as she was helping herself to a third.

'I've been watching you,' he said slowly. He'd come up behind her with a stealth that made Erin jump. Now he placed a hand on Erin's wrist as she turned to slip unobtrusively from the table. Her intention was to disappear under the shade of the oak trees, find a quiet place to sit and enjoy her booty in private. 'Is this your third serving?'

'Yep.' Erin grinned, unabashed. 'The pavlova's finished so I'm having to make do with what I can find.'

'Where on earth do you put it?' Mike asked on a note of pure disbelief. His eyes perused Erin's slim, taut figure, from her trim ankles up.

Erin blushed.

'Beats me.' She smiled self-consciously. 'My mom says I have hollow toes.' She gestured with a laden spoon to the table. 'And this is fantastic. No wonder you're marrying Caroline.'

'She's done a great job. Erin, why are you standing on your own? Come and let me introduce you to—'

'I've met everyone,' Erin said flatly. 'Thanks, Mike, but I'm happy. Please… I'll finish my dessert and then return to be inspected by a few more people.'

Mike's face tightened. 'There's no need to be critical. Erin, if you told these people you'd won silver at the Olympics…'

'They'd be nicer to me,' Erin agreed cordially. 'I

know. Why do you think I don't tell them?' Then, as
his face grew darker, she smiled and shook her head.
'I'm sorry, Mike. Let's just say I like indulging my food
passion in private. Mike, please…I'm happy here by myself. You should be with Caroline.'

Mike's eyes roved across the lawn to where Caroline
was entertaining a group of young men about her own
age. As Mike looked across Caroline turned and saw
him—and saw who he was talking to.

The smile on her face died as she turned back to her
friends.

'I'd go to her if I were you,' Erin advised softly. 'I
don't think Caroline approves of the company you keep.'

'That's nonsense.' Mike sighed—then lifted a bowl
from the table. 'There's King Island cream here, Miss
O'Connell, which appears to have escaped your notice.
If you work on it you can add another five hundred calo-
ries to that helping, no sweat.'

'I had cream on the last two serves,' Erin said blandly.
'I'm cutting it out this time. I have to watch my figure,
you know.'

Mike laughed, and his rich laughter was infectious. It
made Erin smile as well. She ate a spoonful of cake and
watched him with delight.

She'd been talking polite nothings until her face
ached. It was so good to have someone to laugh with.

The memory drifted back of a lonely fourteen-year-
old—and a handsome, smooth twenty-year-old sweeping
the fourteen-year-old out to the dance floor and making
her laugh.

This was a different Mike. A different Erin.

Wasn't it?

'Honest!' Mike was still grinning. 'All the women
here are telling me how delicious the food is and hardly
eating anything. How on earth do you do it?'

'I'll tell you how she does it.' It was Jack, coming up
behind them both. He gazed down at his granddaughter's
laden plate with approval. 'She doesn't stop for breath,

this lass doesn't. Do you want me to tell you what she's done this morning?'

'Grandpa…'

'I will, anyway,' Jack growled, ignoring Erin's protest and talking directly to Mike. 'She was up before dawn checking the cattle. When I woke at six she was down on the flat mending a fence the beasts had broken in the night. She had it fixed before I got there. Then she took Paddy out for a gallop before breakfast, raced in for a slice of toast and raced out because the vet was coming to see to one of the steers; he'd ripped his flank on the broken fence. Then she started clearing out the empty hayshed, and she'd been working like three men 'til I dragged her away to come here. Maybe that's why she's hungrier than the rest of these…' Grandpa's head swivelled round and his face told clearly what he thought of the company. 'These women.'

Then Jack sighed, and his shoulders sagged a little. 'I'm about beat, Erin girl. I think I might take myself off.'

'I'll take you home,' Erin said with alacrity. It was harder for Jack to be here than it was for Erin. He'd come looking forward to a chat with a few local cronies and found no one he knew. Grandpa hadn't learned the defences in this sort of company that Erin had.

Mike's easy laughter faded. He looked from Jack to Erin and back again and his face showed that he understood.

'I'm sorry,' he said softly. 'I didn't choose the guest list.'

'You chose us,' Erin said, forcing her voice to stay light.

'That's right. I did.' Mike looked again at Jack. 'Would you like me to run you home, sir, so Erin can stay?'

'I'll run Grandpa home myself,' Erin said, a trifle faster than she meant. 'I…'

'You don't like my party?'

It was said sadly—like a little boy deprived of a treat—and Erin's eyes flashed up to his.

There was that dratted laughter again—lurking.

Two could play at that game.

'It's a very nice party,' Erin said primly. 'Thank you very much for having us. Can we have a piece of cake and a balloon to take home?'

'What, no lolly bag?' Mike flashed back, and Erin choked on laughter.

'If there's one offering…' She smiled.

'I bet…' Mike turned to where Caroline stood with her friends, twenty yards across the garden. 'Caroline, did we do lolly bags?' he called.

There was an immediate, deathly hush.

The group Caroline had been talking to turned as one—and stared straight at Erin.

Erin flinched.

'I beg your pardon?' Caroline's soft tones echoed across the lawn. 'What do you want, Michael?'

'Lolly bags.' Mike grinned. He had the attention of everyone on the lawn now. 'It's supposed to be a birthday party, isn't it? My guests were just wondering where the cake and balloons were.'

'Whose birthday party?' Erin asked into the ominous hush, and Mike's grin deepened.

'Mine, of course,' he smiled. 'My very own thirtieth birthday party. But I'm not allowed to have presents because Caroline says nice people don't.'

'Don't have presents?' Erin said faintly.

'Don't want them.' Mike smiled. He watched Caroline come across the lawn and stretched out his hand to take hers as she arrived by his side. Around them, to Erin's relief, the murmur of conversation resumed. 'See, Caroline?' he said plaintively. 'I knew we'd be caught out. No lolly bags, balloons or birthday cake.'

He laughed down into his fiancée's eyes—and Caroline managed to dredge up a smile in return.

'Honestly, Michael… You're such a kid.'

'Not me,' he said virtuously. He motioned to Jack.
'It's Mr O'Connell who wants balloons, isn't it, sir?'

Jack twinkled.

'A party's not a party without them.' Then he met
Caroline's eyes and his smile died. 'Not that…I mean,
it's a fine party, miss.'

'There is a birthday cake, though, isn't there,
Caroline?' Mike demanded, and Caroline nodded.

'Of course I've made you a birthday cake.' She smiled
sweetly. 'It's coming out at four…'

'But our guests are leaving now.'

'What, already?' Caroline brightened visibly. She
smiled from Erin to Jack. 'What a shame.'

'So we can't have my cake until four?'

'The catering's organized, Michael…' There was a
strong warning grip on Mike's arm which neither Erin
nor Jack could fail to notice.

'Then there's no choice. You'll have to stay, then, Mr
O'Connell,' Mike said firmly. He removed Caroline's
hand gently from his wrist, and there was a hint of steel
in his voice. It seemed this party definitely wasn't all to
Mike's liking. He took Jack's arm. 'Four o'clock is less
than an hour away, sir,' he said. 'Has Erin told you of
our thoughts on harvesting your hay?'

'Yes.' The old man cast a dubious look across at Erin.
'It seems a generous offer…'

'Generous of Erin,' Mike told him. 'Not generous of
us. Now… Dan's out the back. You know Dan—my
foreman?' Mike looked thoughtfully at Caroline, a frown
behind his eyes. 'Dan doesn't feel all that comfortable
at my birthday party either, so what say I take you round
to drink my birthday beer and settle what paddocks you
cut first?'

Jack hesitated.

'Go on,' Erin said softly, seeing Jack's eyes light up.
Jack had cut himself off almost completely from his
neighbours over the past few years, and his first outing
with Erin shouldn't be marred by Caroline's social am-

bition. Erin smiled at him. 'I might even come with you,
Grandpa. We can drink beer together.'

'I'll take you round,' Mike said promptly. He placed
his wineglass on a trestle table, looked dubiously at his
fiancée and gave a rueful smile. Then he took Erin's arm,
as if making a choice.

'I wouldn't mind a beer myself.'

He didn't stay, of course.

Mike wasn't permitted such a luxury. He settled Jack
into a fold-out chair at the back of the shed, fetched Dan,
started the conversation between the two men and then
excused himself.

Dan and Jack were kindred spirits who'd known each
other for years. There was no need for Mike's presence
to get a conversation rolling.

'I'd better get back to playing host,' Mike smiled. 'I'll
get the rounds of the kitchen table if I don't.'

He was only half joking.

'Do you want to stay or will you come back to the
marquee with me?' he asked Erin.

'Absolutely I want to stay,' Erin said promptly—so
promptly that Mike laughed.

'Not a social butterfly, then, Miss O'Connell?'

'My wings are tired.' She smiled. 'Call me when the
birthday candles are lit.'

'No need. With thirty candles all blazing at once
you'll feel the heat from here. I hope Caroline's organized the fire brigade to stand by.' Mike hesitated for one
more moment. 'Sure you'll be happy here?'

He didn't seem to want to leave.

The machinery shed was full of tractor and truck and
farm bike. It smelled of grease and loose fodder. And
there was the farm's poultry—hens, ducks and the odd
goose—scratching round hopefully on the dusty floor.

It felt great.

Much better than the white satin marquee.

'I'm fine,' Erin smiled. 'But Mike—where are the twins?'

The twins.

Mike looked blankly round.

'Beats me…' Then his brow cleared. 'I know. Caroline's sent them for an afternoon nap. They always have one at this time.'

'An afternoon nap…' Erin frowned. 'But…they're six years old. Surely they don't still need one?'

'I'm sure they do,' Mike said easily. He looked over to the house, upward at the second storey. 'They go up there without a peep every afternoon—and it's great knowing where they are for a change.'

'If you locked them up permanently you'd always know,' Erin said slowly. There was no mistaking the caustic tone in her voice and Mike's face closed.

'Miss O'Connell, are you an expert on children?' Mike McTavish's tone was angry.

'No, but—'

'Then let's admit Caroline might just be right,' he said softly. 'Let's butt out of what's not our business.'

'Just because Caroline's bossy doesn't mean she's right,' Erin muttered. She glared. 'Which is their room?'

'The one over the last elm,' Mike told her. He looked up at their window. 'See? If they were awake surely they'd be at the window. They're good kids. They do as they're told. Now, if you'll excuse me…'

He left them then, returning to his birthday celebration with a frown stamped on his face.

And Erin frowned, too.

She turned to Mike's foreman.

'You know, if I had an Aunt Caroline downstairs, I might just be a good child, too,' she said slowly. 'Poor kids… Do they really stay up there every afternoon?'

'For two hours,' the foreman said grimly. 'They're supposed to sleep from three to five. I've been here a couple of times when they've tried to come down early. Her ladyship hits the roof.'

'Ugh!'

'They won't be asleep,' Dan said sagely. He shrugged. 'I was up on the roof last week—fixing some iron—and had to put the ladder up past their window. They were both lying on the beds staring at the ceiling like stuffed dummies.'

'You're kidding!'

'I'm not,' Dan told her. He shook his head. 'I've never had kids of my own—but it doesn't seem right.'

'It sure doesn't,' Erin said savagely, and started walking out through the shed door.

'Here, Erin…where the heck are you going?' Jack asked in alarm, but Erin only turned and put her finger to her lips.

'I'm just going visiting, Grandpa.' She smiled. 'Ask no questions, you'll be told no lies.'

It took two minutes for Erin to shimmy up the tree. Erin O'Connell had been climbing trees since she was three years old and it was a skill she'd never forgotten.

It was too bad about her dress, though. A shirtwaister with a full-circle skirt wasn't exactly tree-climbing uniform. She managed not to rip it—but by the time she reached the twins' bedroom there were a few branch stains across its soft fabric.

'Too bad,' she muttered to herself. 'The guests here think I'm some sort of lowlife anyway. All I need to cement their impressions is a sherry bottle in a brown paper bag and a good swagger.'

She grinned to herself, hauled herself up the last branch and stopped dead.

The twins weren't asleep.

They were in trouble.

Holy heck… Erin stared, entranced.

On the bedroom floor between their matching pale blue bedcovers was the biggest mound of pastry Erin had ever seen in her life.

Pastry…

It wasn't just pastry. To be precise, it was profiteroles—small round cream puffs almost three inches in diameter. The floor was covered with a vast jumble of small round balls, with what appeared to be toffee and cream liberally adorning all.

And the twins...

The children were sitting on the floor among the mess and their faces wore identical expressions of horror.

Erin tapped on the glass and they nearly jumped out of their skins.

Matt was the first to recover. The small boy slowly rose to his feet, picked his way through the mess of pastry and hauled the window open. Wherever his fingers touched the woodwork became solidly coated with toffee and cream.

'My goodness...' Erin swung herself inside the bedroom, trod on a profiterole and blenched as cream squelched out the sides. 'Good grief!'

'Erin.' Matt gulped. He looked down at the mess and his face crumpled. 'Erin, we don't know what to do.'

Erin stared around. The mess was indescribable. Pastry, cream and toffee—and two children thoroughly mixed in.

It was too much. Erin stared down at Matt's horror-filled face and it was all too much for her self-control. Erin struggled as hard as she'd ever struggled for anything to keep a straight face—but she lost it completely.

A delicious chuckle broke loose, and then another. The children stared up at her, open-mouthed, and the next second Erin had two armfuls of sticky, cream-covered children held close.

'Oh, you crazy, crazy kids. How ever did you manage...?' Erin held the twins away from her and then, at the look of horror still on their faces, pulled them back again. 'Oh, kids...'

'It's not funny, Erin,' Laura murmured into Erin's breast. She'd been sobbing, but somehow, in the face of Erin's laughter, the sobs had changed to hiccups. 'Oh, Erin, we're in such awful trouble.'

'Well...' Finally Erin separated herself from her sticky armfuls to survey the mess without giggles. She sat on the bed—with a profiterole or two squishing underneath. 'Would you...would you like to tell me what happened?'

Laura glared.

'Only if you promise to stop laughing.'

Erin grinned. 'I might,' she said cautiously. 'But I can't promise. I find I always laugh when my bottom's squashing cream puffs.'

'Erin...'

'Okay....okay...' Erin schooled her features into mock seriousness. 'I'm all ears—as long as no cream puff finds its way into my ear holes. Tell me.'

'Well...'

This, it seemed, was the birthday cake.

Erin nodded wisely as the sad tale unfolded into her sympathetic ears. Erin had seen cakes like this before—only never in such a jumbled form. The cake was called a *croque-en-bouche*, she knew. The last one Erin had seen was a vast pyramid of profiteroles standing about four feet high and glued into delicious elegance by strands and strands of golden toffee.

A *croque-en-bouche* made by an expert was a joy to behold, Erin knew—and she also knew just how tempting such a sight would be to two bored six-year-olds.

'We were going to miss out on it completely,' Laura said sadly, searching Erin's face for signs of anger and judgement. 'Aunt Caroline told the caterers the cake was to be served at four, and at three o'clock she still said we had to have our afternoon sleep. We weren't allowed to come down until five. So me and Matt decided we'd just look... And it was sitting all by itself in the dining room and it was so high we thought it wouldn't hurt if we took just one cream puff from the bottom.' She looked anxiously up at Erin. 'The ones at the bottom had most toffee, you see, and we thought Caroline would notice if we took a top one.'

'I do see,' Erin managed gravely, only a faint twitch around her eyes betraying her enjoyment. 'And what happened then?'

'Then…then it sort of collapsed,' Matt quavered. 'All over the top of Laura. And we didn't know what to do so we got a big tray from the sideboard and we carted it all up here to try to fix it.' He looked despairingly around. 'Only it won't go together.'

'No.' Erin's lips gave a very obvious twitch. 'I see that.'

'You're not allowed to laugh,' Matt reprimanded her, and Erin fought it back.

'No.'

'We're in trouble.'

'I can see that, too.'

Her laughter died. As Erin thought it through she winced. Maybe Mike would laugh. In fact Erin was almost sure Mike would laugh. Caroline, though… Caroline she wasn't at all sure of.

Or maybe she was. Maybe she knew that, with Caroline, the kids were in for a really hard time. Hmm…

'What are we going to do?' Laura asked anxiously, and four eyes gazed at her with absolute dependence.

'We…'

Erin, it seemed, had been placed very firmly on the twins' side.

'Can you put it together, Erin?' Matt asked anxiously.

Erin looked round the room. Squashed cream puffs from door to window.

'No.'

Matt gulped. 'Then…then I guess we'll get into really bad trouble.'

'Not necessarily,' Erin said slowly. 'You know, kids, what we really need here…' She paused.

'Yes?' Four desperate eyes, and a word spoken as one.

'What we really need,' Erin said with decision, 'is a fall guy.'

'A fall guy?'

'Well, maybe two fall guys.' Erin grinned. 'I wouldn't want one fall guy to face your Aunt Caroline alone. Okay, kids, let's mobilize.' She looked at her watch. 'With luck we have thirty minutes before anyone comes looking for the cake. Let's move!'

CHAPTER EIGHT

MIKE found them at four-fifteen.

From where they sat, Erin and the children had listened to the fuss downstairs with fascinated horror.

There had been one long scream of fury, and then heaps of shouting—and one yelp. The twins and Erin felt guilty about the yelp.

They waited for angry feet to pound up the stairs—but no one came.

They waited on. The children giggled and giggled, and Erin started getting very, very nervous.

She hoped it was Mike who found them rather than Caroline.

And finally Mike came.

They heard his knock on the twins' bedroom door, and then his call as he found it pristinely clean—maybe a little damp—but empty.

'Laura… Matt… Where are you?'

There was enough concern in Mike's voice for Erin to nudge the twins.

'Call back,' she said. 'Tell him where we are. And remember. We know nothing!'

Laura stifled yet another giggle, looked at Matt for courage and opened her mouth.

'We're in the bathroom in the spa, Uncle Mike,' she called gamely. 'With Erin.'

'With…'

There were fast footsteps on the landing, the bathroom door was wrenched open and Mike McTavish appeared in the doorway.

And stared.

'What the…'

Six eyes gazed innocently up at him from a sea of foam. All three were neck-deep in bubbles.

The spa was huge. It was built to seat four or more, and Erin and the small twins took up less than half its capacity. The spa was sunk into the tiled floor of the bathroom and the floor around them was awash with foam.

'I tipped too much bubble mixture in.' Erin smiled at Mike apologetically. 'I'm sorry. Don't yell at the kids. It was my fault.'

Mike took two steps into the room and stopped dead.

'What,' he said slowly, his eyes not leaving Erin, 'are you doing in my spa?'

'Erin's never been in a spa, Uncle Mike,' Matt faltered. 'She…she wanted to know what it was like.'

'Erin…'

'Erin came up to visit us,' Laura said quickly. 'Wasn't that nice of her?'

'Very nice,' Mike said automatically, but his eyes showed sheer amazement. He carefully looked at each of them in turn—Laura, Matt and Erin—and made a discovery.

'You're all still dressed…'

It was too much for Matt. The little boy choked on laughter and dived under the bubbles.

'We couldn't get into the spa in our nothings,' Erin said virtuously, meeting Mike's stunned look with limpid innocence. 'I didn't have a swimming costume and there are gentlemen present.'

'Gentlemen?' Laura choked.

'That's Matthew,' Erin informed her kindly. 'But, Matt, if you don't stop tickling my toes I'll stop calling you a gentleman. Surface immediately!'

Mike McTavish stared. Then he pulled a chair out from the wall and sat down hard.

'I don't think Caroline will like this,' he said heavily.

'Then I think you should tell Caroline that the twins were simply entertaining a visitor,' Erin said, meeting his look with defiance. It was pretty hard to look defiant, though, when she was neck-deep in bubbles. 'I came up to visit the twins, they showed me the spa and I asked to have a go. So, what else could polite children do?'

What else indeed?

The corners of Mike's mouth twitched. The movement was almost imperceptible, but Erin saw it—and knew they were home dry.

Well, home wet!

'We heard a scream downstairs,' she said innocently. 'Has something happened?'

Mike's eyes were slowly turning thoughtful.

'You could say that.' He met her eyes and their look held.

Erin's colour started rising—and she struggled so hard to keep her face straight it hurt.

'Will you tell us what happened?' she asked again. Like Matt, Erin wanted badly to choke with laughter and dive under the bubbles. Somehow she made herself stay straight-faced.

'A small disaster,' Mike said slowly. 'Gastronomically speaking.'

'Oh?' Both twins were studiously regarding bubbles, their faces so innocent they were dead give-aways. Erin kicked them both under the foam—and Matt subsided into giggles again.

'The farm dogs ate my birthday cake,' Mike announced, in tones as solemn as the grave. Like Erin, he seemed to be having trouble schooling his facial features.

'They didn't!' Erin's eyes widened in horror. 'What, all of it?'

'Enough.'

'Oh, no,' Erin said solemnly. 'And it was such a magnificent cake.'

Silence.

'How,' Mike said carefully, 'do you know that my birthday cake was magnificent, Miss O'Connell?'

Erin bit her lip.

'Mr McTavish,' she said, with the same careful tone he'd used, 'how could your thirtieth birthday cake, made by your very own cordon bleu-trained fiancée, be anything but magnificent?'

Their eyes stayed locked. Erin's colour was brilliant crimson. She descended a bubble or two, with only her nose and eyes above the foam.

'I…I see.'

And she knew that he did.

'Did…did the dogs get into trouble?' Laura asked breathlessly.

'Yes.'

'Very much?' Matt's voice was even more anxious than Laura's.

'Well, let's just say Blackie yelped when Caroline threw something at him.' Finally Mike allowed himself to grin. 'Only, when Blackie realized what she threw was a cream puff, he turned and wolfed it before making off to his kennel. I guess I now have two farm dogs unfit for anything more than a slow waddle for days and days.'

'Oh…oh, dear,' Erin said faintly.

'The thing we can't figure out is who let them in.' Mike's gaze went from each in turn and finally rested again on Erin. 'You didn't let them into the house when you came in to visit the twins, I hope?'

'Who, me?' Erin demanded in an injured toned. 'No way.'

'How did you get into the house?'

'I climbed the elm.'

'You climbed…' Mike's voice faded to silence. He simply stared.

'That's why I don't mind hopping into the spa with my clothes on,' Erin said kindly. 'I made my dress dirty climbing the tree.'

'You made…' Mike shook his head. 'I don't believe

this. I suppose now you're going to come downstairs and enjoy the rest of my party in your sodden dress?'

'I shouldn't think so.' Erin smiled. 'I thought I might just shimmy down my tree, collect Grandpa and slope off home. That is, if you have no objection?'

Mike smiled then, a slow, lazy smile that encompassed them all, and from the twins came answering shy smiles of relief.

'I guess…I guess I can't object,' he said softly to them all. His smile, though, gradually became all for Erin, holding her in thrall. 'How long…how long have you all been in the bath?'

'When did you find the birthday cake?' Erin asked.

'About five to four.'

'Well, we've been in here since long before then,' Erin said virtuously. 'Haven't we, kids?'

Mike grinned.

'Well, then, you three innocents…' His smile embraced them all. 'You all must be turning into prunes.' Mike bent and lifted Laura high from the water, set the little girl on her feet and handed her a towel. 'Undress, twerp, leave your clothes here and then off to your bedroom to dress.' Matthew received the same treatment, sent on his way by Mike with an affectionate ruffle of his wet hair.

And then Mike turned his attention to Erin.

'Your turn, Miss O'Connell…'

Erin had sat motionless in her bubbles and watched Mike deal with his niece and nephew. She was suddenly absurdly shy. Her dress felt heavy and clinging in the water and she wasn't the least sure how decent she'd be when she emerged. It *was* such light material!

'I can get myself out,' she managed. 'I'm a big girl…'

'You are not.' Mike laughed down at her and his strong hands scooped her under the arms and lifted. 'A big girl, Miss Erin O'Connell, is what you definitely are not!'

Erin came up from the water in a breathless rush, and Mike held her hard against him to steady her.

'See. Not so big,' he said softly, and his hands still held. And they held her so she couldn't escape.

She should pull away. She should…

Instead, Erin let temptation have its sway. She let her body slip against his, knowing she was wetting him with her sodden dress—and suddenly not caring.

Mike's hands were dropping to her waist and still holding her tight against him in a gesture of protective caring.

'Erin…'

Erin's dress was so wet it hardly existed. She could feel the hard maleness of Mike's body holding her close, and suddenly it was all Erin could do to breathe.

'M…Mike. Let me go…' It was barely a whisper.

'I'm not sure whether I should.' He smiled into her damp curls. 'I'm not sure whether this is one prisoner who should be dragged away in irons.'

'What…what do you mean?' Good grief, it was as much as she could do to whisper.

'My dogs have been by my side all afternoon,' Mike said reflectively, his hands warm and strong about her waist. 'They're loyal, to say the least, and they don't leave me. But… At about ten to four I heard a whistle coming from round the house. Both dogs took off to investigate—and didn't come back. Next thing I know, they're up to their whiskers in my birthday cake. Strange, wouldn't you say, Miss O'Connell?'

'Very strange…'

It might be strange, but what had happened to the dogs was a lot less strange than what was happening to Erin's body at that exact moment. Erin felt washed and warm—and really, really odd.

As if she was where she was always meant to be.

Held by Mike McTavish.

'I only know one person who can whistle like that,' Mike said softly into her ear, and Erin managed to smile.

He missed her smile. Erin's smile was turned into his chest. But he could sense her laughter.

'You must hang out with the wrong birds,' she managed. 'I... In the circles I move in, bird calls like that are quite common.'

'In the circles you move in...' Mike shook his head. 'What circles, exactly, are those, Erin O'Connell?'

'Nice circles,' she said definitely. 'My Grandpa. My Mom and Dad. The twins and Paddy.'

'Where whistling is normal.'

'Absolutely.'

'I see...' There was a long pause. The silence stretched out, endless between them. Erin dripped steadily onto the floor but neither Mike nor Erin seemed to notice.

All Erin noticed was her heart, thumping away like a battering ram within her chest.

'There are wet splodges on the children's beds,' Mike said at last. 'Like something's been washed. How are you intending to explain that?'

'Wet splodges?' Erin did pull away from Mike then, her bright eyes laughing up at him with mock indignation. 'Well, what do you expect, Mike McTavish? You just sent two soggy children into their room to towel-dry and dress.'

'They were there before.'

'Nope.' Erin shook her head with absolute conviction. 'They can't have been. I'm sorry to have to correct you, but you must be mistaken, Mr McTavish.' Then she paused. 'Or maybe...or maybe I sent Matt back in to find a rubber duck—and he dripped...'

'Erin...'

'Yes?' She dimpled up at him, held at arm's length but still held for all that.

Mike stared down at Erin's laughing face and his mouth twisted into an expression that wasn't quite a smile. It was the look of a man who wasn't quite sure what was happening to him.

'You are one crazy, crazy woman, Erin O'Connell,' he said at last. 'You've been here less than a week—and my nice, ordered life is being turned upside down.'

'No!' Erin made her face mock-desolate. 'Is it? I hope you're not blaming me.'

The woman was incorrigible!

'I was particularly looking forward to my birthday cake,' Mike said bitterly.

'Well, so you should have been,' Erin twinkled. 'It was delicious. If I were you I'd ask Caroline to make you another.'

'Erin…'

'Yes?' She twinkled up at him—but all of a sudden the twinkle died. There was a look in Mike McTavish's eyes that precluded laughter. There was a look in his eyes that Erin would have died for ten years ago—and now she didn't know how the heck to respond.

She knew how she wanted to respond.

She knew how her body was responding.

Erin's body was responding with the most basic of woman's needs. The need to let herself be held by the man she loved…

Her eyes met Mike's and it was as if she was drowning in their troubled depths. His eyes devoured her—a man hungering for something beyond his reach—and Erin knew his body was giving him the same message hers was screaming.

Good grief…

She could feel his need…

And this man was engaged to be married to Caroline Podger. A suitable wife…

He was still engaged. There was nothing but trouble for Erin O'Connell in this man's arms.

So Erin O'Connell was going to have to find strength to haul herself out of reach.

And somehow she did.

Somehow Erin pushed herself back, shoving her hands against Mike's chest and pushing herself out at arm's reach. Then somehow she hauled herself completely out of his grasp, grabbed a towel and backed to the door.

He didn't follow. He stood, looking at the sodden girl before him as a man might look at a dream.

'M—Mike…Mr McTavish, if you'll excuse me,' Erin said softly, and her voice was so unsteady she wasn't sure he could understand what she was saying. His face looked confounded. 'I'm…I'm leaving. Thank you for the party. It was great.' She managed a shaken smile. 'I haven't enjoyed a party so much for a long, long time.'

'But…' Mike took a hasty step after her but Erin was too fast. She was already out of the door. 'Erin…'

She didn't stop, backing fast into the twins' bedroom. By the time Mike reached the bedroom door Erin was already at the window.

'Where do you think you're going?' Mike demanded, his voice unsure.

'I told you.' Erin smiled at the astounded twins and then swung one dripping leg over the sill. 'I'm going down a tree.'

'You can't!'

'Watch me,' Erin said simply, and launched herself out into the wide branches. Her handhold safe, she turned to smile at all of them. 'If I were you,' she advised them kindly, 'I'd clean the bathroom. And I'd change your shirt, Mike McTavish. You're all soggy down the front. And if Caroline finds bubbles over the floor—well, who knows what unjust accusations might be made?'

CHAPTER NINE

MIKE and the twins cleaned the bathroom in conspiratorial silence.

Afterwards, Mike changed his shirt, settled the twins with Snakes and Ladders and returned to his party—but his heart wasn't in it.

The afternoon was drawing to a close. Caroline was graciously bidding her guests farewell and Mike moved to do the same, automatically responding to their social niceties.

'Happy birthday,' they told him.

Happy birthday…

This was his thirtieth birthday and he had to pinch himself to believe it. Erin O'Connell had accused him of sounding about eighty—and that was how he felt.

He'd decided he wanted a life like this, Mike told himself firmly as he stood beside Caroline and smiled until his face ached. In Mike's childhood his mother had put on social afternoons just like this. The farm in his mother's day had been gracious and welcoming—a hub of social activity. Margaret McTavish had been a charming hostess and a good mother—and the twins had the right to the same sort of lifestyle their father had enjoyed.

That was Caroline's role.

Provider of a stable childhood. Wife and mother…

'Did you like your party?' Caroline asked as the last guests disappeared into their BMW and waved a bright farewell.

'Of course.' Caroline was standing right beside him and Mike put his arm around her waist—but only because it seemed the right thing to do. The gesture was expected, but his heart wasn't into hugging Caroline.

It had to be. This was his life from now on, he reminded himself sharply. Expected. Planned. Controlled.

The sort of life where kids could grow up knowing what was expected of them.

Until last week this had seemed the only solution to the twins' upbringing. Why, now, was it starting to look so bleak?

'I'm sorry about your birthday cake, Michael, darling,' Caroline said sadly. 'I was so angry. One of the caterers must have left the door open—even though they all deny it.'

'It can't be helped.'

'If I could just prove it was down to their carelessness we could deduct something from their pay.'

'I doubt we'll ever prove who it was,' Mike murmured, thinking of the pristine bathroom upstairs and the bundle of wet clothes and towels in the laundry basket waiting for Mrs Brown in the morning.

Mrs Brown could keep a secret.

Caroline flicked a look at her watch. 'The twins have been good.' She smiled approvingly. 'Almost five and not a peep out of them.'

'I went up before to check,' Mike told her. 'They were reading and a bit bored. I popped them into the bath and put them in their pyjamas.'

'You didn't…' Caroline frowned. 'While our guests were here…'

'They were feeling a bit left out, Caroline,' Mike said heavily. 'I don't think they enjoyed my party very much. Maybe…' He sighed. 'Maybe it wouldn't have hurt to let them come down for the birthday cake.'

'If there had *been* a birthday cake,' Caroline said bitterly. 'Blasted dogs…'

The two dogs behind Mike slunk back a few paces, eyeing Caroline warily. They sensed Caroline's dislike—but they were a bit too full of cream puff to do much about it. The younger one gave a small, defiant wag of his tail.

'Today was a celebration,' Mike was saying heavily. 'To leave the twins out of things seemed a bit unfair…'

'It's their routine,' Caroline told Mike, her voice definite. 'Children must have a routine. All the books say so.'

'Yeah?'

'Look, they'll be at boarding school next year,' Caroline went on. 'They'll have to be used to a routine then.'

'I guess you're right.' Mike sighed again and whistled his overfed dogs back to his heels. 'I'm going for a walk, if you don't mind, Caro. I'll be back in an hour or so.'

'Don't call me Caro, Michael,' Caroline snapped. 'You know I hate diminutives.'

'So you do.' Mike nodded. 'Okay. Caroline is fine by me.'

Only it wasn't.

Caroline wasn't fine by Mike.

She had to be fine. Caroline was his fiancée, for heaven's sake. He should be out walking round the wheat fields thinking of Caroline…

Instead, all Mike McTavish could think of was one crazy slip of a green-eyed girl called Erin O'Connell.

Mike took his dogs down through the vast wheat crop, following the path that Matthew and Paddy had cut the other day. They'd flattened a trail with their mad gallop.

'Little twerp,' Mike thought ruefully, remembering the sight of his small nephew on the huge horse—but he couldn't make himself angry.

Nor could he make himself angry over one ruined birthday cake.

He knew darned well who was responsible for ruining his cake, but all Mike McTavish could do when he thought of his niece and nephew—and their accomplice in crime—was to smile.

Especially when he thought of their accomplice in crime.

One Erin O'Connell.

Mike McTavish had lifted Erin O'Connell's slight body from the spa and something had happened to him that Mike McTavish hadn't had happen to him before in his entire thirty years.

Mike McTavish had felt out of control.

The memory of Erin's soft body—how it had yielded deliciously under his hands and nestled against his body—flooded back to him and his smile slowly slipped.

It had been a wonderful feeling to hold her....

Erin's body was so slight. So soft. So...

So perfect!

This was crazy!

'You're being ridiculous, McTavish,' Mike told himself soundly, and the dogs gazed up at him in concern. They weren't used to the boss talking to himself.

'Yeah, I know. I aided and abetted a crime.' Mike grinned down at them. 'I stood back and watched while you guys got into trouble, and now I'm talking to myself.' Mike grimaced. 'Go on, then. Slope off home—just like Miss O'Connell. See if I care...'

The dogs looked doubtfully up at him and moved a little closer—as if guarding their off-balance master. Mike's grin returned. The dogs' opinion was transparent. He was crazy, their look said, but they loved him anyway.

He couldn't turn yet to go back to the house. Not yet...

Mike kept on walking, up over the hill and down towards the river. If he kept walking he'd come to the O'Connell boundary...

Maybe Erin would be out riding Paddy...

'Go home and help Caroline clean up,' Mike told himself savagely, and tried to make his feet turn. They wouldn't.

Caroline didn't need him, he knew. She'd be bossing

the caterers to her heart's content—and she didn't appreciate a man in the kitchen.

She didn't appreciate her routine being interfered with one bit.

'And that's why you're marrying her, Mike McTavish,' Mike told himself sternly, ignoring the worried look of his dogs. 'You're marrying the woman because she's predictable. She's competent and eminently eligible. She knows what I want in a wife. What *do* I want in a wife? Someone to look after the twins.'

It had never gone past that, he acknowledged as he thought back over his decision. The twins had been thrust on him and he'd panicked. And now...

'Now it's taking some getting used to,' he muttered. 'Domesticity...'

It wasn't just domesticity that was taking some getting used to. It was also Caroline's ideas on what their life should be like. The entertaining and organization...

'My parents entertained,' he told the dogs. 'All the time. It's what married couples do.'

He couldn't remember his parents' parties being like Caroline's orchestrated function this afternoon, though. He remembered people enjoying themselves...

'And I don't remember being sent to my room...'

For heaven's sake... What he was thinking was close to heresy. Caroline had come into his life when he was overwhelmed and she'd lifted an almost unbearable responsibility from his shoulders. He should feel nothing but gratitude.

Instead Mike could think of nothing but Erin.

There was a dark shadow on the horizon, moving fast.

Mike slowed to a stop.

It was Erin. There was no mistaking horse and rider. They were galloping over the far O'Connell paddock, girl and horse moving as one. Erin O'Connell... He could see her chestnut curls flying wild and he wondered vaguely whether her hair would still be damp.

He wanted to touch those damp curls...

Erin O'Connell...

The slip of a girl was no higher than his shoulder, on a horse too big for her...

Erin O'Connell was a girl with a heart so big it took in the world. It took in Laura and Matt and Jack O'Connell...

What sort of a girl would give up international competition and the reputation of a world-class horsewoman to save her grandfather's farm? he thought, his mouth twisting into a wry smile.

What sort of a girl?

A crazy one.

He'd be honoured to call Erin O'Connell his friend, he decided, knowing he'd move heaven and earth to get her hay harvested for her.

Was it enough?

Of course it was enough. What else was he thinking of?

It was only the remembrance of Erin's slim, yielding body that was his undoing...

'And you can shove feelings like that away with your bachelorhood,' Mike told himself savagely, his eyes fixed firmly on the distant flying horse and rider. 'What sort of a life would I have if I ditched Caroline and formed some sort of relationship with that...with that...?'

He couldn't describe her. He couldn't think how to describe Erin.

'I'd have three children, that's what I'd have,' he said bitterly. 'Three madcaps, running wild. And Laura and Matt have to be brought up right. They're my responsibility and I have to see it through.'

So...

So there was no more to be said. No more to be thought.

Mike McTavish cast one more long look at horse and rider—as one might hold desperately to a lingering dream—and then he turned to go back to the house.

He had responsibilities waiting. He had his life carefully planned. Things were mapped out. Life was under control.

He turned to go back to Caroline.

CHAPTER TEN

IT WAS more than time for hay-carting.

Monday was clear, calm and hot—late summer weather with a forecast of nothing but heat on the horizon for the next week. Erin listened to the forecast over breakfast, and as she finished her toast Mike and Dan arrived in convoy.

Today's task was mowing. Erin had assumed she'd be using Jack's old tractor with its ancient cutter, but both Dan and Mike were on huge, modern tractors with vast hay slashers on the side. With this machinery they could cut both paddocks in a day!

For Erin to use Jack's outdated mower was just plain silly. It'd be like a tadpole swimming alongside a whale!

Erin gave Jack a call to let him know what was happening and walked out to the verandah to meet them.

To meet Mike...

Why on earth did he always make her feel like this? she wondered as she pushed open the screen door. As if she wanted to turn tail and flee—because she had no way of stopping the twisting pain inside her heart.

'Morning, Miss O'Connell.'

Mike McTavish swung his long legs down from his tractor and loped up the verandah to meet her. He glanced at the watch on his bare, sun-bronzed arm. 'Or is it still morning? Eight a.m. Almost lunchtime.'

'I'd given you up,' Erin teased, trying to ignore the effect his muscular body in its hip-hugging jeans and torn, open-necked shirt was having on her. 'I thought you were waiting for a bit of cool.'

'Not us. The hotter the better. Weather like this is made for hay-carting—or for the beach, depending on

your level of indolence.' Mike motioned to where Dan
sat on the second tractor. 'Jack said yesterday we should
cut the river paddock first. We're off to do that now so
we'll see you this evening—unless Jack has any last-
minute instructions...'

This evening... They were intending to cut the hay
without her.

Another long day without Mike...

'But what about me?'

Erin shoved her hands in her jean pockets and bit her
bottom lip. Whoops! She hadn't meant to sound like
that. Her voice had sounded exactly like a child missing
out on a treat.

Mike had heard the similarity and grinned.

'You can come down and watch if you promise not
to get in the way,' he said generously.

Erin screwed up her nose in distaste. Ignoring Mike,
she stalked down to the second tractor. 'Dan, do you
have something else to do this morning?' she asked
nicely, and Dan smiled doubtfully down at her.

'Well, there's always the odd hundred jobs...' He
glanced uncertainly at his boss and then back to Erin.
'But your hay takes priority. You're late cutting it now,
miss. It should have been in the shed a month ago or
more.'

'Yeah, but I can cut as well as you can,' Erin told
him bluntly. 'If you'll trust one of these tractors to me.'

'Erin...' Mike came down fast to stand behind her.
He put his hands on her shoulders and gripped. 'What
are you playing at? Do you think we'd let a woman do
our work...?'

Hmph! The feeling of his hands on her shoulders was
almost enough to make Erin swallow her indignation—
but not quite.

'Are you saying I can't cut straight?'

'You can cut real neat, I'll bet.' Mike grinned down
at her. 'Or maybe in nice ordered patterns...'

'Herringbone,' Erin agreed snidely. The feel of

Mike's hands was sending shards of heat right down her shirt. She pulled away and turned to face him. 'Honestly, Mike, I can do this as well as you and Dan—and I want to. It's our hay. It means you or Dan can stay home and I won't have to feel so guilty.'

'Erin…'

'You can both come back for the baling,' Erin promised sweetly. 'We need three for that—and Grandpa's arthritis has been giving him a hard time so I'll need you both.'

'He's not well?' Mike asked, frowning up to the verandah. There was no Jack in view.

'Grandpa's just tired,' Erin told him. 'He had back pain in the night and didn't sleep. It's settled now so I've persuaded him to stay where he is.'

'Tell you what, boss,' Dan said generously, looking from Erin to Mike and back again, with a faint smile playing behind his eyes. It was as if he sensed there was something between these two, and intended to encourage it to the full. 'Why don't I borrow Miss O'Connell's truck and take myself home? I can get that tank cleared like we'd planned if Miss O'Connell's willing to take my place. Good idea?' Then, before Mike could reply, Dan was off the tractor and holding his hand out to Erin. 'Your truck keys?'

His eyes were giving her an urgent message. Do this fast, his eyes said.

Erin handed the keys over, bemused, and Dan took off under the trees to where the truck was parked.

'You might ask whether it's fine by me!' Mike yelled after him.

'What's fine? Working with me or working with Miss O'Connell?' Dan grinned back at him and gave Erin a broad wink. He was already in Erin's truck, gunning the motor into action. 'Jeepers, boss, a man'd have to be a sandwich short of a picnic to keep me beside you—when you have this alternative!'

The truck grunted into gear and departed with speed.

Mike and Erin were left alone.

'What the heck…?' Mike stared after him, bemused. 'I wouldn't have said that tank cleaning was that important!' His eyebrows snapped down into a frown. 'Interfering…'

'How is he interfering?' Erin demanded, and Mike shook his head.

'Dan doesn't like Caroline,' he admitted. 'If he thinks he's playing matchmaker…'

'He can't play matchmaker when you've already made your match,' Erin managed, and only she knew the effort it cost her to say the words.

'No.' Mike's face was still thunderous. He shook his head and then turned to face Erin. 'And I also wouldn't have thought,' he added slowly, 'that you'd want to leave your grandpa alone if he isn't well.'

'Grandpa's fine alone,' Erin reassured him. She managed to smile up into his still angry face. 'I think…what you have to realize, Mike, is that Grandpa's been on his own for twenty years. Me singing round the house all the time is a shock. He likes it—but a few hours on his own is a welcome change.'

'Do you sing?' Mike asked, and Erin's smile widened.

'Of course. All the time. Don't you?'

'Not…not a lot. What do you sing?'

'Nothing you'd want to hear,' Erin said promptly, her smile widening. 'Actually I don't think it's what Grandpa wants to hear either. I sang Handel's 'Messiah' in the shower this morning, and when I turned off the water Grandpa'd put the radio up loud enough to drown me out.'

Mike shook his head, a preoccupied smile starting to play around his eyes.

'You're nuts, Erin O'Connell,' he told her firmly, anger fading. This girl was half-woman, half-bewitching elf—and Mike's foundations were starting to seem just a bit shaky. Or maybe… Maybe very shaky indeed. 'It'd be a brave man that ever took you on,' he said slowly.

'Then it's just as well I have Grandpa,' Erin flung
back at him, tilting her chin and meeting his look with
defiance. 'And it's lucky he's not so nice in his require-
ments as you, Mike McTavish. Now... Shall we hit the
hay?'

'There's nothing I'd like better,' Mike said solemnly—and all of a sudden Erin was burning with em-
barrassment as the *double entendre* hit home like a
sledgehammer.

And so, it seemed, was Mike McTavish.

That was the last time they talked for the morning.

They could have split and each cut one of the two
vast paddocks of dry grass, but by silent consent they
decided to work in tandem. They slashed side by side,
Erin's tractor slightly behind Mike's, cutting straight
along his slash line. This way took more concentration
but it was far more fun than cutting alone.

More fun?

Erin was so conscious of the man in the next cab that
her hands stayed clenched hard on the steering wheel all
morning.

The heat shimmered down on the golden hay. Erin
concentrated fiercely on her driving, knowing she was
being judged and refusing to let Mike McTavish gain a
march on her. If he increased speed, so did she, forcing
herself to always be only feet behind his tractor.

She succeeded magnificently. By midday the first paddock was flattened, the slashed hay lying in the hot sun
to dry. Three days of sun and it'd be ready to bale, Erin
thought with solid satisfaction. This lot baled meant she
had feed for the winter, plus some to sell...

The last row complete, she cut the engine of her tractor and jumped down as Mike's came to a halt beside
her.

Erin's huge tractor had been vibrating her body all
morning, and jumping down onto firm ground was like

coming onto dry land after months at sea. Her body kept vibrating—and the land didn't.

Whoa…

Erin's legs sagged beneath her and she caught at the tractor to stop herself falling.

'Erin…' Mike was down before her. He took two fast steps forward and caught the swaying girl, steadying her with strong hands. His hands gripped her waist and held hard and he smiled down into her stunned face. His smile held concern. 'Not as capable as we thought, are we, Miss O'Connell?'

'I'm capable…' Erin tried pulling away from his hands, but her legs didn't quite work. Not yet. Strangely, the feel of Mike McTavish's hands wasn't helping her steadiness one bit. 'I'm…I'm just hot.'

Mike produced a vast handkerchief—and Erin subsided into it gratefully. Mike still steadied her waist. Erin's face was dripping perspiration—and her flushed appearance wasn't entirely due to the feel of Mike McTavish's hands. Not entirely…

'I should have stopped before this. We need air-conditioned cabs,' Mike said ruefully, looking down with concern at Erin's heated face. Mike's tractors were fitted with roll bars and weather hoods but were open to the air. 'We have air on the combine harvester.'

'Lucky wheat cutters,' Erin managed. 'It's a pity this is hay and not wheat.'

'It is that.' Mike looked closely at her. 'You've had enough. Do you want me to call Dan to do this afternoon's cutting?'

'No.' The refusal sounded ungrateful, but Erin was darned if she was admitting to weakness. 'I can cope. I…I wouldn't mind lunch, though. Will you come up to the house and have a sandwich?'

'Will Jack mind very much if we don't?'

Erin tried to make her hot brain think. Her hot brain wouldn't get past the feel of Mike McTavish's hands…

'No,' she managed at last. 'He's…Jack's so used to

making his own he often eats before I get there anyway. But...' She hesitated. 'I think I do need half an hour's rest,' she admitted.

'Mighty concession,' Mike teased. He looked down at Erin's face in concern. 'Are you sure you can go on?'

'I'm sure.'

He nodded, as though expecting no less, and a warm glint of admiration flicked through his smile. 'An hour's rest would be more like it, then,' he decreed. 'And an hour out of this sun. Let's go down to the river.'

'I should have brought sandwiches...'

'No need,' Mike said cheerfully. 'Our Mrs Brown was on duty early this morning and here's everything we need.' He relinquished his hold on Erin's waist with lingering regret, reached up to behind his tractor seat and hauled out a cooler. 'Lunch is served, ma'am,' he told Erin. He caught her hand and held it fast. 'Can you walk as far as the river?'

The river was just at the base of the paddock they were cutting. Cool gums edged the riverbanks, and from where she stood in the blazing sun Erin could almost hear the water's soft rippling.

'I can walk that far,' she said with quiet dignity. She hauled her hand back but couldn't regain it without a fight—and she had no strength left for fighting. 'For a river...for a river I could almost run.'

It took two minutes of hot walking across the slashed wheat to reach the point where the land sloped down to the river.

Here the land hadn't been cleared, and gnarled gums spread their blessed canopy of shade across the slow-moving sweep of water.

The river looked magnificent. Erin paused at the top of the bank and drew in her breath at its loveliness—at the broad sweep of bank and the shallows rippling over sand—and then the cool, deep roll of currents beyond.

'We should have brought our swimming gear,' Mike said ruefully beside her. He looked doubtfully down at the girl at his side—and Erin knew just what he was thinking. If she hadn't been here, he'd have had his clothes off and be into the water so fast...

And so would she. She couldn't swim in heavy denim jeans and leather boots. If Mike weren't here...

Well, she was darned if she was missing out on a swim just because he was male and she was female.

It wasn't just that he was male. It was because he was Mike McTavish that she was hesitating...

Ridiculous!

'I'm darned if that's stopping me,' she said definitely, her voice surer than her thoughts. 'Not the way I feel. My backside feels on fire from sitting on that plastic seat, and the rest of me's not much better.'

'Erin...'

'Let me go, Mike McTavish,' she ordered, halting her hand from his clasp. 'I have more important things to do than dally here with you.'

Then, before Mike could answer, Erin had kicked off her boots, hauled her jeans down and off and was running down to the water.

Erin was still more respectable than in a bathing costume, with her oversized shirt hanging below her hips, but she was self-conscious enough—until she hit the water.

Her feet hit the shallows, she took a running dive and her body knifed down into delicious, cool water.

As a sensation it took a lot of beating. It was magic. The cool washed over her like a blessing, removing dust and grime and pollen in one fast sweep. The hay band holding back her hair came free and her hair streamed out around her in chestnut ribbons.

Blessed release...

She sank deeper. She was running out of air and she'd have to surface soon.

On the surface Mike McTavish was watching...

Well, she couldn't stay underwater for ever. Erin was a strong swimmer, but every swimmer had her limit! The

last of the air in her lungs trickled out and Erin turned
her face upward to sunlight.

She broke the surface to find Mike still exactly where
she'd left him—holding the food cooler and watching
her as one might watch an alien from outer space.

'What are you doing on dry land?' she flung at him,
breathless from being underwater for so long. 'The
water's fabulous.'

'I don't…' The man seemed absolutely nonplussed.

'Don't what? Don't swim? Well, get in the shallows
and splash!' She twinkled across at him from the centre
of the river, threw a huge spray of water in his direction
and then knifed her body down once more into the
depths.

When she surfaced, Mike McTavish was no longer on
the bank.

Erin took three deep breaths and looked around—and
then disappeared again under the water.

It wasn't voluntary.

She was being dragged down by two strong hands—
dragged down until her toes hit the sandy bottom—and
then released to bounce upward like a cork from a bottle
of fizz.

She surfaced, laughing and choking all in one.

'Oh, you rat fink…' Mike's head came up behind hers
and she twisted round in the water to face him. 'How
dare you? I might have drowned…'

'Not you.' He grinned. Water was streaming down his
face, and his eyes were so close their noses almost
touched. 'You're a water rat yourself. I've never seen
anyone hit the water with more enjoyment…'

He reached out through the water as if to touch her—
but Erin knifed away.

All of a sudden Mike McTavish was too darned close.
Too darned close by far for a man engaged to someone
else!

She couldn't stay near him. She couldn't!

Erin turned into the current, resolutely away from

those laughing eyes. Then she launched herself strongly up the river against the flow, her shirt hindering her hardly at all. All she was conscious of was that some-where behind her was Mike McTavish.

He was very close...

Gradually Erin became aware of him, his body just slightly behind and to the side of her, his head at about the level of her waist.

This man could surely swim. He was pacing her and she was swimming at her maximum strength. Each ounce of extra effort Erin put in, he matched stroke for stroke.

And gradually Erin's tension eased, and she swam with him as one...

It was a weird sensation. Wonderful...

It was as if they were dancing. It was as if she was being held. Each time Erin's hand sliced through the water, she felt Mike's arm come down at exactly the same moment, and she felt the wash from his powerful shoulders sweep across her thighs.

She shouldn't be doing this. She shouldn't. This man was engaged to be married to someone else.

They were only swimming.

They were not, Erin acknowledged to herself. At least, she wasn't. What Erin was doing here was falling deeper and deeper in love with the man beside her. She was falling in love with his very presence.

What Erin was doing was becoming one with Mike McTavish.

One body. One life...

This was crazy. Crazy!

A log loomed ahead, fallen down over the river to make a rough, rotten bridge. It blocked their way com-pletely.

Almost thankfully Erin somersaulted into a turn—and let the current carry her back.

She didn't know whether Mike was following. She didn't care. All she knew was that she no longer had him stroking at her side. She could no longer feel him as a powerful surge of skill against her body.

And finally she again reached the place where Mike had left the lunch cooler. Erin turned and pulled herself into the shallows—and then watched Mike drift down after her.

Mike must have stopped by the log for a moment—giving her a chance to get ahead.

Giving her a chance to get free.

Did he feel what she was feeling? Erin wondered dully. He couldn't. He couldn't feel like this and stay engaged to Caroline Podger.

She hauled herself to her feet on the sand, pushing her streaming hair back from her eyes, and watched Mike come to shore.

'You beat me.' He smiled as he surfaced from the last stretch. He rose to his feet and Erin gasped in shock.

Unlike Erin Mike had left his jeans on—but that was all. His chest was gleaming bare and wet.

It was the sort of chest one saw in the worst type of women's magazines, Erin thought ruefully. The sort of chest her mother had always told her that 'nice girls' didn't look at. 'Nice girls' weren't interested in that sort of thing!

Nice girls mightn't be interested. Erin, frankly, was. She couldn't look away.

And Mike stopped dead.

He stared at Erin—and then looked downward to where she was looking.

'Have I left my fly undone?' He grinned, his sun-burned face deepening a tinge.

'Nope.' Erin pursed her lips and made herself look away. 'It's only…'

'Only what?'

Erin hiked over to the cooler and opened the lid—just to give herself something to do. Just to give her something to look at besides Mike McTavish. 'Do you lift weights?' she muttered.

'Nope to you,' Mike smiled. Erin was fumbling with the cooler catch. He walked across to her and bent to flick it up. It came free at his touch. 'I grew these pecs all by myself,' he admitted, still smiling. 'There's the odd million hay bales behind any muscles I have.' He drew back and looked down at her kneeling figure. 'You're an odd woman, Erin O'Connell. I didn't think nice girls commented on men's bodies.'

It was so close to what Erin herself had been thinking that she almost gasped. She plonked herself down on the sand, lifted a sandwich from the cooler and bit into it— just to give herself time to answer.

Mike didn't follow. He stood looking down at this strange, child-like woman on the sand, and his face creased in uncertainty.

Erin ate three mouthfuls of the sandwich before she found the courage to talk again—and then she glared.

'Aren't you eating?'

'I'm enjoying watching you eat. I've never seen a woman enjoy eating as much as you.'

'You've been moving in the wrong circles,' Erin muttered darkly before she could help herself. 'With women who don't notice men's bodies. Women who pretend to not enjoy eating.'

'That includes nearly every woman who was at my birthday party,' Mike said slowly, and Erin took another savage bite.

'That's right, Mr O'Connell,' she told him. 'You move in the wrong circles.'

'Erin…' His brows snapped down hard.

'I'll eat the lot if you don't start,' she warned him. She waved a sandwich at him. 'They're very good.'

'I'll bet they are.' The black look gradually faded. Finally Mike lowered himself onto the sand and took a sandwich for himself. 'Okay, Miss O'Connell. Let's get our batteries restoked and see what else you're capable of on a tankful of fuel! Mowing, swimming, insulting… Is there no end to your talents?'

CHAPTER ELEVEN

WHAT Erin did on a tankful of fuel was sleep.

She ate her last sandwich, drank her third glass of lemonade and then closed her eyes in the dappled sunlight while she waited for Mike to finish.

She woke an hour later.

Mike was touching her shoulder.

For a moment Erin froze. Mike was lying beside her on the sand, his hand now lightly on her arm. Their faces were a foot apart—or less!

'Time to get back to work, sleepyhead.' Mike was smiling into her confused eyes. 'Unless you'd like me to call Dan...'

'No...' Erin scrambled to her feet, suddenly absurdly conscious of her missing jeans. She looked round frantically for her mound of abandoned clothes—and Mike threw her jeans over to her.

'Time to get decent,' he grinned.

'I...'

'I know.' He hauled himself up as well, pulling his shirt over his brown skin. 'You'd rather cut hay naked. It gets a bit itchy, Erin, believe me.'

'Have you tried it?' she flung at him, and he grinned.

'I can't say I have. I've always had more sense.'

'And you don't think I have any sense at all,' Erin said slowly, meeting his look. 'You think...you think I'm a little bit crazy.'

'A little impulsive,' Mike said softly. 'But you're young...'

'Meaning I'll grow out of my nonsense?'

'Well...' Mike sighed. He buttoned his shirt and

turned to pack the cooler. 'One day you'll wake to find the world asks a price.'

'A price for silliness?'

'I guess…' He paused and then straightened, looking down at Erin's perturbed face. 'I guess we have to face our responsibilities eventually. Sometimes…sometimes it's so darned sudden.'

'Like it's been for you,' Erin told him softly. 'You have the twins now—so you've put away silliness. Put away childhood. Embraced responsibility with Caroline…'

His face closed. 'Don't let's bring Caroline into this.'

'Do you love her?' Erin asked—oh, so casually—and could have bitten her tongue out as soon as she'd voiced the words.

They were impossible to retract. They hung between them as some dark cloud over the heat haze of the day. The cloud wasn't cool and shading, however. It was oppressive in its darkness.

'Erin…' Mike's hand came out and took her wrist and a grim smile played around his lips.

Erin didn't fight his clasp. Instead she stayed motionless, looking down at the joining of their two bodies, wrist to hand.

'Yes?' She forced her eyes up to meet his and her voice was a breathless whisper.

'Erin…' Mike gestured as if he would release her—and then thought better of it. In one savage movement he pulled her against his body and held her hard. 'Erin, this is crazy.'

'What…?' She was held against his heart and his hold was taking her breath away. Her heart stilled almost to a stop. 'What's crazy?' she whispered. 'You holding me?'

'What we feel…'

And Erin's heart kick-started again.

So he felt it, too. It wasn't just her.

This emotion wasn't just silly imaginings left over

from ten years ago. This was something between man and woman—something that happened over and over again—a feeling as old as time itself.

A feeling so precious it was like gold. Better. A thousand times better…

But Mike was shaking his head into her damp, tumbled hair.

'Erin, I can't…'

'Can't what?' She could feel his heart under her breast. Her breasts were crushed against the hardness of his chest and she gloried in his feel. 'What can't you do, Mike McTavish?'

'I can't have any sort of relationship with you,' he whispered. His hands held her hard, giving the lie to his words. 'Erin, I'm not young and single any more. I have responsibilities.'

'So you do.' How hard to make her voice work!

'You do see, don't you?' He pushed her away and held her at arm's length, still not finally relinquishing her. 'You must see, Erin. The twins are my responsibility now. A huge responsibility. I have to bring them up as their parents would have wished. They need the right…the right…'

'The right mother,' Erin supplied, even though it was a physical hurt to say what he was thinking. 'By the right mother, you mean Caroline.'

Caroline.

The name hung between them. Caroline hung between them.

'It's what their parents would have wanted,' Mike said heavily. 'Marrying Caroline will work. She's organized. Sensible. Stable.'

'And from the right social circles,' Erin said before she could stop herself, and Mike nodded slowly.

'I… It's important that she knows how to behave. How to teach the children. That we bring the children up to—'

'To be sensible,' Erin said bitterly. 'Boring. Nicely

brought up little socialites. I'll bet Laura will never be allowed to comment on a man's pecs.'

'I guess she won't.' Mike gave a wry grin. 'I'll see to that. Or rather, Caroline will.'

'I'll bet,' Erin said savagely. 'Let me go, Mike McTavish...' They were still chest to chest, and Erin's heart was pounding so hard Mike must surely feel it.

'Not until I've made you see.' Mike's grip on Erin's wrists tightened. 'Erin, I've been wanting to say this since the night I came over to your farm. I wanted to say that if I was free... God knows it's a stupid admission, isn't it? But if I was free...if you'd come three months ago...before all this... You and I...' He shrugged. 'Well, we could have had fun.'

'You mean you would have had an affair with me,' Erin said carefully.

'I would have wanted to,' Mike smiled. 'You're a very desirable woman, Erin O'Connell.'

'But you wouldn't have married me?'

'Hell, Erin, I wouldn't have thought of marriage,' Mike said honestly. 'I hadn't thought of marriage then and didn't intend to for years. I mean...marriage isn't an indulgence. It's not something one does because of a momentary whim.'

'No,' Erin said softly. 'It's not, is it? What is it that the marriage service says? Something about entering into it reverently...'

'That's just it, isn't it?' Mike muttered savagely. 'Reverently... There's nothing in the marriage service about marrying because of fun and passion. Marriage to you... Marriage to someone like you would be crazy. Fun for a while...until the responsibilities took over...'

'As they surely would,' Erin agreed gravely. 'The moment you expected me to cook.'

Mike caught his breath and stared down at her. His grave eyes lightened a little at her look and the smile behind his eyes threatened to return.

'You're laughing at me...'

'It's either laugh or cry,' Erin said softly. 'And...and I've always preferred to accept life's responsibilities with laughter instead of tears. Giving up my position in the national equestrian team, leaving my parents... You're not the only one with hard decisions to make, Mike McTavish. You treat me like a—like a fluff-headed flibbertigibbet. Here today, gone tomorrow. And I think...' She took a deep breath. 'I think what you're saying to me is insulting.'

'I don't mean to insult you.'

'Saying I'm the sort of woman you'd have an affair with but not marry is pretty darned insulting,' Erin whispered. 'You're telling me I'm from a lower order...'

'I didn't say that.'

'What are you saying?'

'Well, you can't cook for one,' Mike said, exasperated. 'The twins and I would starve to death!'

'So live on sandwiches. Or—horror of horrors—learn to cook yourself. Maybe we could have lessons together. It might...it might just be fun—but there's your dreaded fun word again, Mike McTavish. And who knows? Having fun just might not kill any of you.'

'But—'

'But what?' Erin threw at him, and then drew back in horror. Good grief. It was almost as if... This was almost as if she were proposing.

'Erin...'

Erin's bubble of laughter was impossible to find now. It was gone completely. There was nothing but silence hanging over them, a silence so vast it threatened to overwhelm them.

'Are you saying you'd marry me,' Mike said slowly, 'if...if I asked?'

Erin closed her eyes, searching for courage.

Surely she couldn't be honest. Surely she had more pride than to tell this man the truth.

It wasn't possible to be anything else but truthful.

Finally Erin's clear green eyes opened and she looked up at her love, pain twisting round her heart like a vice.

'Mike McTavish, I've loved you now for ten years,' she said softly. 'You asked me to dance ten long years ago and I fell in love with you on sight. I hoped...I hoped it would have ended, but you see...you see it hasn't ended at all. I love you still. If you asked me to marry you...' She sighed and pulled away. 'If you asked me to marry you, though, I'd say no.'

'You'd say...'

'You don't want me as your wife,' Erin said simply. 'You don't think I'd make the grade. And neither I would. I couldn't meet your expectations and I'd break my heart trying. So... So I think it's time you went back to your Caroline and got on with your life. That's what I think.'

This time the silence was almost deafening.

'Hell,' Mike said at last, and Erin nodded.

'It is,' she said simply.

'Erin...'

'There's no need to say anything,' she whispered bleakly. Their hands were still linked, for all the world as if they were two lovers. 'And I shouldn't have said anything either. You don't—you don't need me in any shape or form, Mike McTavish. I just thought...I just thought that, seeing I've never fallen in love before—and maybe I never will again—that maybe you had the right to know. For what it's worth.'

Her voice trailed off to miserable silence.

'Erin...' Mike's voice was full of wonder. 'Erin, what you're offering me...what you've already granted...it's a gift...'

'One you don't want.'

'One I might well have wanted. In a different time. In a different place.' Mike pulled her hard against him and swore into the silence. 'If it was just for me...'

'It's not for you, though, is it?' Erin said. 'It's for the twins and it's for your position as a pillar of society.

Wealthy landowner. You have to marry a suitable wife. And I'm not it.'

'No.' The word was rough and painful to hear. 'Erin, you keep mocking my social status and that's ridiculous. But the twins and their upbringing... That's not ridiculous.'

'Of course it's not,' Erin flashed at him, and then subsided. 'Please, Mike, let's... Let's get back to work. Let's forget this ever happened.'

'I can't...'

'You must,' Erin said softly. 'You must.'

Mike swore again—and then pushed Erin back a little from him. For a long moment they stood motionless, the pain reflected in each other's eyes.

Their faces were so close.

Unbearably close.

So close that, inevitably, there was only one thing to do. One thing that both knew was right...

Slowly...slowly Mike's mouth came down on hers, and Erin's face tilted up to meet him.

And their lips joined.

One body...

Only, of course, they were no such thing. No wedding vows had welded these two into one.

Erin shouldn't have let him kiss her.

There was the grim, sensible Erin who should have screamed blue murder and run. She should have taken off from here as fast as her bare legs would take her. Escape the present wonder to avoid future pain.

Instead she did no such thing. Erin raised her face to meet Mike's—and the sensation was just as she'd always dreamed it would be.

It must be the heat making her feel like this, she told herself desperately—the heat and the fact that she'd just woken from heavy sleep. There was still a dreamlike quality about it.

But the feel of Mike's lips on hers wasn't a dream. The feel of his strong farmer's hands holding her body close, and the warmth and flickering desire behind his laughing brown eyes…

No dream…

The tenderness caught and held her more strongly than any ties of steel. The feel of him caught at the memories of an Erin at fourteen years old—lonely beyond belief in a strange country and finding solace in those eyes—and there was the ghost of fourteen-year-old Erin in the way she responded.

But it was only a ghost.

The real Erin was very much a woman. No childlike response this… The real Erin was lifting her hands to hold Mike's head closer—her arms in her still damp blouse pulling Mike's body closer…closer. The real Erin was parting her lips to deepen the kiss—and welcoming Mike McTavish into her heart with every vestige of her body.

Here was her peace.

Here was her home.

But, of course, it wasn't.

The kiss couldn't last. The sweetness was an illusion. A moment's madness on Mike McTavish's part—infinitely wonderful but only fleeting. It had to end. The pain was starting for Erin even before she felt his body stiffen. Before she felt him regain sanity and know that this was madness.

And finally he did. Finally Mike was pushing Erin back from him with hands that were unsteady and dark eyes that were creased with trouble.

'Dear God, Erin…' Mike's voice was husky with unspent passion. 'Erin…I'm sorry…'

It needed only that.

He was sorry.

A flash of anger came to her rescue. Not much—but enough.

'S—sorry for kissing the chambermaid while the wife's not looking?' Erin whispered. She dragged her eyes from his and took a step back, right out of his grasp. 'So—so you should be.'

'Erin…'

'I'm not—I'm not in the market for a casual affair, Mike McTavish, even if you can forget you're marrying someone else.' Erin closed her eyes. 'Now…if you've quite finished, let's get back to work—before I say something I may well live to regret.'

Mike looked at her for a long moment with those dark, troubled eyes, and then finally bent again to finish packing the cooler.

'Get yourself dressed, then, Erin,' he said heavily. 'You're right. There's work to do and we…we're wasting time.'

The next paddock was cut differently.

Without discussing it, Mike and Erin went back to work, but, by mutual unvoiced agreement, they cut from opposite ends of the field.

They didn't meet until the paddock was completely flattened, and even then it was only to say a formal goodnight and arrange transport home.

To Erin it felt as if she were saying goodbye for ever.

CHAPTER TWELVE

IT WAS three days before Erin saw Mike again.

They seemed like three lifetimes.

Which is ridiculous, she told herself harshly. You're behaving like a silly teenager with a crush.

Silly? Crazy more like. How crazy could she get? To expose herself so completely... To say she loved him... You're a fool, Erin O'Connell, and that's a fact, she told herself over and over again.

The inner lectures didn't make her feel one whit better. In fact, they made her feel worse.

The twins came and went for their riding lessons, and reported events from the McTavish household without being asked.

'Mike and Aunt Caroline spent all last night writing wedding invitations,' Laura told Erin sadly. 'And I can't be flower girl because Caroline says she only wants one bridesmaid and that's her stupid sister. Erin, if you ever get married, can I be flower girl?'

'You sure can.' Erin smiled, but her heart knotted in a twist of self-pity at the thought. Erin getting married... Impossible. Not when she'd given her heart so utterly ten years ago—and it had never been returned.

The hay-carting started in earnest on Thursday. Mike was there—but somehow Erin hardly seemed to see him. He brought three of his men, which meant they had all the hands they needed in the paddocks. Erin stayed in the haystacks, hauling bales higher and higher under the hot tin roof until the sheds were crammed to bursting.

By the time Mike brought the last trailer in, late Friday, Erin was more tired than she'd ever been in her life. And satisfied to boot.

Jack had been overseeing the whole operation, pottering back between hay shed and paddock with increased delight, and he'd ridden his horse down to close the gates as the men went home—so Erin was alone as the last trailer came in.

So, for the first time since Monday, she was alone again with Mike McTavish.

Mike had been working in the paddocks, baling for the past two days, sending the trailer-loads of stacked bales back to the home hay sheds with his men. He'd eaten lunch in the paddock with his men as well—while Erin had eaten at the house with Jack.

Maybe she should have joined the men's lunch down at the river. One half of her had wanted to. The other half had been afraid.

Now, as dusk fell on the final day, she looked down to find Mike McTavish at the wheel of the tractor bringing in the final load. And her stomach knotted in tension.

She'd stopped expecting Mike McTavish.

'Do you have room for one more load up there?' Mike called.

Erin was as high as the rafters. From where she stood Mike appeared tiny.

'Just haul the elevator along to this end,' she called. 'Send 'em up. I'm ready.'

There was no more talk for fifteen minutes or more as Mike heaved the bales onto the elevator and Erin lifted them from the top and carted them to their position in the stack. It was hot, heavy work, and she was desperately glad to see the last bale in position.

She walked back to the edge of the stack—but, before she could look down, Mike McTavish's long form hauled itself over the edge and up to join her.

'Finished,' he sighed. He perched on the edging bale and looked down onto the yard.

Mike was as tired as Erin was, she thought. His voice sounded drained—and Erin felt a moment's compunction.

'You've done too much.'

That made him turn. He swivelled so he was looking back through the gloom under the rafters, trying to see.

'You've done all the work here by yourself, though,' he said slowly. 'Heaved two thousand bales in two days. And you say *I've* done too much!'

'I enjoyed it,' Erin confided. 'And the men have been helping. Sending the men back in pairs meant I wasn't completely by myself.'

'Your pecs will be as big as mine any day, no sweat,' Mike teased, his eyes still wondering. He shook his head. 'Heaving that many bales…'

'Two thousand,' Erin said with quiet satisfaction. She hesitated, and then, because she seemed to have no other option, she moved out and came to sit on the edge beside him.

The farmyard was spread before them. In the distance Erin could see her grandfather cantering peacefully down towards the river. Even from here she could sense the lightness in the old man. The relief. This hay safely under cover meant the farm was still a going concern.

Mike's men were packing up the machinery and wending their way homeward. Job well done.

The farm was a financial proposition again, thanks to Mike McTavish.

'I…we're very grateful,' Erin said shyly. She twisted to look at him but Mike was concentrating on the speck that was her grandfather and his horse.

'No need.'

'There is a need.'

'The twins are loving their riding lessons,' Mike said, still not looking at her. 'Matt's a different kid. He bounces round the house. And the only thing that makes him grumpy is being told we're baling and you won't have time for a lesson today.'

'He's had three lessons this week.' Erin smiled. 'He's hardly deprived. You know, Mike, he promises to be very good.'

'It's a great skill for a kid to have,' Mike agreed. He seemed not to be speaking to Erin. Mike seemed almost to be speaking to himself.

It was as if he was afraid to look at her.

'I loved riding as a child,' Erin said gently, easing the silence. 'I always had a friend. First my Toby, and then Peace—and now Paddy.'

'Your friend, Paddy,' Mike said heavily, and he finally swivelled to look at her. 'Lucky Paddy.'

It was said with gentle irony—and Erin didn't know whether he was mocking her or not.

Discomfiting, all the same.

'I should go down,' she told him, her voice hesitant. 'I...I need to cook dinner.'

'You? Cook?'

This time there was no mistaking the irony and Erin flushed.

'There's no need to make fun of me, Mike McTavish.'

'I just feel sorry for your grandpa.'

Erin bit her lip. It was almost as if he was being deliberately rude. As if he was trying to make her angry...

He was succeeding.

'Yeah, well, don't bother,' Erin snapped. 'There's more important things in life than cordon bleu cooking, in case you hadn't noticed.'

'So what are you having for dinner?'

'It's none of your business.' Erin's green eyes flashed wrath. 'You're just judging me against Caroline. Holding me up to ridicule...'

'I'm not...'

'What are you doing now, then?' she demanded, and Mike had the grace to stay silent. 'See,' Erin said bitterly. 'You can't deny it. Caroline's perfect—and I'm the "also ran". The one who might have got the prize if you'd just been out for a bit on the side.' She rose unsteadily to her feet, stooping a little to fit under the roof. 'I'm going down. You can stay here all night for all I care...'

'Erin…' Mike's hand came out to catch hers—and Erin jerked back. She couldn't bear this. She couldn't bear him to touch her.

'Let me go, Mike McTavish.' It was meant to come out angrily. Instead, it came out as a breathless, hopeless plea.

And her plea was answered from another direction.

'Erin…!'

The yell broke through Erin's anger and uncertainty. It was as piercing as any whistle—impossible to be ignored.

The twins…

Mike swore slowly—and let Erin go.

'Are you both up there?' Laura yelled. 'Mrs Brown said we could race over and get a ride back with Mike. Can we come up?'

'If you can climb,' Erin yelled down to them, avoiding Mike's eye. She was almost overwhelmingly grateful for their presence, and the next moment, as two small noses appeared over the top, she could have hugged them.

They weren't interested in hugs. The two urchins were enthralled with the stacked hay.

'Wow! This is fantastic!' Laura gasped, looking round at the vast mound of golden bales. 'What a great place for a cubbyhouse. You could almost live up here. We don't get this at our place, do we, Matt? 'Cos Mike puts his hay into big rolls.'

'It's the way of the future,' Mike said serenely, greeting niece and nephew with affection. 'But our Erin's a nice old-fashioned girl…'

'Whose grandpa doesn't hold with vast hay rolls you can't lift,' Erin finished for him, her colour still higher than she'd like. 'And neither do I. If we used rolls we'd have to buy all sorts of expensive handling equipment…'

'So you'll use one green girl instead.' Mike frowned as the twins started inspecting the weird, wonderful place under the high tin roof. 'Erin, your grandpa's beyond heaving hay bales.'

'Then it's just as well I'm not beyond it,' Erin said abruptly. She turned to the bale-hopping children. 'I hope you two have come to collect your uncle for dinner.'

'We have.' Laura grinned. 'And we hoped he'd give us a ride home on his tractor. But…' She looked doubtfully from Erin to Mike. 'We don't have to go home quite yet—do we, Mike?'

'Oh, yes, Mike does,' Erin said firmly, and her heart echoed the sentiment.

She just wanted Mike McTavish somewhere else. Somewhere distant enough for her heart to settle to normal pace.

'You're telling us to go home?' Mike said softly, his eyes holding a look Erin didn't understand, and she gritted her teeth and made herself answer.

'Yes, Mike McTavish,' she managed. 'I'm more grateful than I can say for your hay-carting—but for now…for now I want you to go home.'

Five minutes later Erin was free to do something about dinner.

She fumed as she did so.

Mike McTavish thought she was hopeless. He thought she was hopeless just because she couldn't cook!

She could cook, she thought bitterly, if she followed the instructions slowly and with care. It was only that her thoughts kept racing off at a tangent. Cooking never seemed worth concentrating on.

Okay, so try!

She tried, and by the time Jack O'Connell appeared from the river paddocks there was a passable tuna bake sitting on the table—with a salad beside it.

Jack stopped dead at the door, his nose wrinkling in appreciation.

'Hey…'

'I'm not as useless as you think,' Erin said firmly, meeting his eyes with defiance. 'I can cook.'

Jack frowned. 'I've never said you were useless, Erin girl,' he growled. 'And I never would. Not once in a million years.'

'Yeah, well, I burned the chops last night...'

'Well, Sadie loved your chops. The old dog reckons you're the best thing since sliced bread—and there's nothing wrong with the fried eggs we ended up eating.' Jack walked across to his granddaughter and gave her a solid hug. 'Now... What's been upsetting you enough to try cooking?' He grinned down at the laden table. 'It must be pretty bad to warrant a casserole *and* a salad.'

'It's not...' Erin swiped a hand across her face as an errant tear streaked down through the dust on her face. 'It's only... Why does Caroline Podger have to be so dratted competent?'

'She's not.'

'She sure has everyone fooled, then,' Erin whispered. She hugged Jack back. 'I'm sorry, Grandpa. It's only...it's only...'

'It's only that you're still in love with Mike McTavish. Isn't that so, girl?' Jack O'Connell sighed. 'It's no good, Erin. There's no joy in that direction.' He stamped across to the sideboard and handed Erin a gilt-edged card, elegant tinted ivory with raised gold lettering.

Erin read it through with eyes that blurred. She knew already what it would say: *...the marriage of Caroline Alison Podger and Michael Lyon McTavish...*

Erin stared at the invitation for a long moment, fighting back an almost overwhelming compulsion to burst into tears.

'Will...will we go?' she whispered.

'I guess we should,' Jack said sadly. 'I'll have to haul the suit out of mothballs. But we're to be neighbours for a long time, lass.' He cast an anxious look at his granddaughter. 'Seems we'll have to make the most of a bad job.'

'I guess…' Erin plonked herself down at the table, her appetite gone.

'I won't enjoy the wedding any more than you will,' Jack promised, still worried. 'It'll be a grand formal occasion, if I know the Podgers. Like that damned lunch only ten times worse.' He grimaced. 'Folks have forgotten how to party, for heaven's sake…'

'That's one thing my parents taught me,' Erin murmured, trying to drive away pain with remembrance of something more pleasant. 'We've always had the most fantastic parties.'

'Your mother put one on here once,' Jack said wistfully. 'Your mother was the best party organizer this side of the Atlantic.'

'And the other side.' Erin smiled. 'She's taught me, too. I've organized a couple of big parties myself, to say thanks to people who supported my riding—and they worked just fine.'

'So you're not as useless as you think, then.' Jack smiled softly, watching his granddaughter's face.

'Not at home. Not in the States. But here…'

'Folks are the same the world over,' Jack said roundly. 'And, Erin, you know it's my eightieth birthday in two weeks?'

'Eightieth…' Erin looked up from contemplating misery and stared. 'Oh, Grandpa. So it is. With the hay-carting and everything it slipped my mind.'

'Now don't say that,' her grandfather begged, an odd look in his old eyes. 'I was hoping you might be planning a party for me.'

'But…do you want a party?'

'I sure do.'

'What sort of party?' Erin asked cautiously, and Jack laughed.

'You tell me, girl,' he said softly. 'You can't tell me what a great organizer you are and then demand I organize things myself. We'll have a bit of spare cash now, won't we, now we can sell a few hay bales?'

'We will.'

'Okay, girl,' Jack announced. 'Go to it. I'll tell you who I want invited—and you organize me a birthday bash.'

It seemed Grandpa wanted half the valley.

Jack O'Connell must have sat up most of the night to do his guest list, and at breakfast Erin was presented with two closely written sheets of names.

'They're all people who I'd like to see here,' Jack told her when Erin stared at the list in stunned silence. 'They're all friends. The old cricket boys. People from church. The chaps from the Returned Soldiers' League, plus any neighbour worth his salt.'

'There's over a hundred names…more, with families.'

Jack smiled beguilingly at his granddaughter. 'Yeah, well… Who knows, girl? This is my eightieth birthday, after all. The next party you organize for me may well be my wake.'

'Yeah, I'll bet,' Erin said bitterly, her dancing eyes giving lie to her harshness. 'Grandpa, this is blackmail. With my luck you'll live until you're a hundred and ten, and I'll be inviting this many people every year.' She read the first few names—and then laid Jack's list down next to her cornflakes. 'Grandpa,' she said carefully. 'Mike McTavish and Caroline Podger are top of the list. And the twins.'

'I want children,' Jack said firmly. 'A party's not a party without kids.'

'But Caroline…'

'As I said, we're going to be neighbours for a long time,' Jack told her. 'We have to learn how to get on. Besides…' His old eyes twinkled with devious mischief. 'It won't hurt young Caroline to learn how a real party's run. It's time she discovered how a proper hostess operates.'

CHAPTER THIRTEEN

WHICH was all very well, Erin thought bitterly, but it sure put her on her mettle.

Erin thought fleetingly of Caroline's fabulous marquee and her team of caterers as she went about her day's work and knew she and Jack couldn't afford that in a million years.

So the party had to be done Erin's way.

They'll think I'm a real country hick, she thought savagely, and then remembered Jack's list and thought again. Jack's list consisted of old men, lifelong friends and neighbours with young families. Lots and lots of kids.

She could give them a good time.

Unconsciously she found herself walking closer and closer to the river.

The river was the perfect place.

Okay, Erin, she said doubtfully to herself, and only she knew how scary it sounded to her inner self. Let's show this place a party where people do more than eat elegant food and sum each other up. Let's have a proper party.

She had two weeks.

Two weeks to Jack's eightieth birthday.

Six weeks to Mike McTavish's wedding.

The two were jumbled in her mind and Erin was aware of a deep mist of unhappiness surrounding her everywhere she went—but at least she could concentrate on the party.

Concentrating on something other than Mike McTavish's wedding was the only way to keep herself sane.

*   *   *

The morning of Jack's birthday dawned clear and hot. The twins burst into the O'Connell farmhouse mid-morning with the force of a small whirlwind.

'Today's Grandpa's party day. Today's Grandpa's party day,' they sang as they aeroplaned across the ve-randah. Jack had been adopted very firmly as belonging to both of them—and Jack enjoyed his two new proxy grandchildren enormously. They burst through the kitchen door and stopped dead.

'Wow…' said Matt.

'Goodness,' breathed Laura.

'Hi, twins.' Erin waved a hand in welcome from somewhere behind more balloons than the twins had ever seen in their lives. 'You're just who I needed. Are you free for the morning?'

'Y—yes,' Matt agreed doubtfully, his eyes enormous. 'Mike said we had to be home by twelve to get dressed for the party—but he said if we weren't a nuisance we could watch things being set up.'

'You can do more than that,' Erin said firmly, emerg-ing from her clouds of balloons. She gestured to the floor in the hall. 'See those boxes? Each one holds a huge pavlova base—a great big round of meringue. I swopped fifty bales of hay for them, so treat them with care. There's ten plates spread out in the living room and a bucket of whipped cream in the middle of the living-room table. Can you put a pavlova on each plate and dollop cream nice and evenly over the tops?' She held up two fingers two inches apart. 'This thick!'

Laura and Matt both stared at Erin, open-mouthed—as if they couldn't believe she really meant it.

'You mean, really help?'

'Really help,' Erin said firmly.

'But it's for a proper party,' Laura said doubtfully. 'I mean…Caroline says we have to stay out of the way because we'll mess things up.'

Erin put her hands on her jean-clad hips and surveyed them thoughtfully.

'Will you mess up my pavlovas?' She smiled. 'If I can leave you to do this I'll go out and pick strawberries to go on top. Grandpa and a couple of his mates are taking trestle tables down to the river, so you'll be on your own. Surely I can trust you?'

The twins looked at each other in wonder and, as one, their small faces turned to the vast bucket of cream in the dining room.

And two small faces broke into incredulous smiles.

'Can you ever,' Matt breathed.

From that moment on, Jack O'Connell's party was a wild, rip-roaring success.

The twins could hardly bear to go home and change—and if it hadn't been for Caroline's angry telephone call demanding their return they would have stayed right on—cream-covered clothing and all.

Therefore it was almost two in the afternoon before Mike McTavish appeared at the river—flanked by the elegant Caroline and two sprucely scrubbed twins.

Erin had been trying like crazy not to watch for them—and failing miserably. She was pouring punch for two old ladies as she spotted them over the riverbank, and it took sheer physical effort to keep herself chatting to her guests.

Mike stopped dead as he topped the rise and stared down about him in absolute amazement. As well he might, Erin thought in satisfaction, looking round and trying to see Grandpa's party as Mike McTavish would see it.

She had balloons everywhere. Erin had spent four hours the night before, with Grandpa's ancient bicycle pump, blowing up the odd thousand balloons, and all the early guests had been handed a bunch of balloons with instructions to spread them imaginatively. Now they were hanging from every available tree in green, white and silver glory, blending in with the vast eucalypts and turning the setting into something that looked magical.

She'd dug two vast pits and lit fires in them, well away from the undergrowth—and roped in a friend of Grandpa's from the local fire brigade to keep watch during the night. A side of beef for a night's duty was a fair price, he had thought. The local butcher had been happy with the same arrangement and had prepared meat for her. Vast sides of beef were now cooked to perfection, and willing hands were carving off more meat than even the hundred or more guests could possibly eat.

Erin watched as Mike's fascinated eyes moved on.

There were no prepared salads.

Instead, Erin had simply supplied ingredients. Jack's trestle tables groaned under vast bowls of lettuce, tomatoes, radishes, celery, avocado, pine nuts, cucumber, hard-boiled eggs, sour cream and cheeses... There were bowls and bowls of garden-fresh produce, with a sign saying 'USE IMAGINATION' and bottles of ready-made dressing at the end of the table alongside mustards and chutneys and pickles.

And bread...

The baker hadn't wanted hay—but he and his wife had just had a new baby, so Erin had promised babysitting services in return. He'd done her proud, and he and his wife and newborn were watching the district scoff their produce with pride.

Further on there were tables of pavlovas. The twins were grabbing Mike's hands and hauling him over to inspect, almost bursting with pride. Erin had handed them the strawberries and left them to decorate at will, so they really were all their own work.

There was music bouncing out around the trees—and Erin watched Mike's eyes widen as he recognized one of his men behind the fiddle. Erin had discovered the farmhand's passion while he'd heaved hay up to her during hay-carting—and when Erin had sent him an invitation he'd approached her with the offer of the band.

'We're just starting up, like,' he'd told her shyly. 'Country music. And...and I know this is going to be big—and the guys and me all have a lot of time for your grandpa. If you were willing to give us a plug…tell everyone who we are, like…'

Erin sure had. She had huge banners strung from the treetops, screaming 'MUSIC BY THE HAYBOY HICKS!' Corny, but fun. There were old men staring up to the trees, wondering how Erin had managed to get the banners so high.

The band was toe-tappingly good. Already they had the kids and a few brave adults organized into line dancing—those kids, that was, who hadn't found the river water irresistible.

The river was a magnet for everyone.

There were guests perched on the branches hanging out over the river and heads bobbing up from the water. The beer barrel was down by the water's edge—with a sallow-faced youth with more pimples than years acting as barman-cum-lifesaver all in one.

The youth had appeared yesterday, selling encyclopedias door to door. He was a student trying to make money for next term. He'd looked lean and miserable—and Erin's one extravagance had been to offer him a day's wages and all he could eat in return for working today.

Now he couldn't wipe the grin off his face—and one of the neighbour's daughters was making sheep's eyes at him from a distance.

Erin grinned at the two of them as she watched. Romance was in the air. Then she finally turned back to Caroline and Mike.

Romance faded.

They didn't have the same look.

Caroline looked appalled—and Mike looked just plain hornswoggled.

They also looked just a little overdressed.

Erin's invitation had stressed 'casual' and most people had taken her at her word. Erin herself wore her habitual jeans and a cool checked shirt. Mike, too, wore denim, but Caroline wore yet another lovely pair of tailored trousers—white, Erin saw with a grimace, and winced again as she saw Sadie go up and sniff, leaving a grubby wet nose print on the immaculate trousers from snuffling at the water's edge.

'Welcome…welcome to our party.' It took an effort for Erin to make herself smile at the pair of them—especially as their hands were linked as they gazed down at the twins' pavlovas—but somehow Erin managed it. She walked across to greet them properly. 'Would you like beer or punch? If you'd like beer, go down and see Eric—but if it's punch you'd like, then I'm your lady.'

'I… Is the punch alcoholic?' Caroline asked faintly, and Erin shook her head.

'Too many kids here,' she said bluntly. 'Besides, it's too darned hot. People drink more than they ought and then they hit the water and we're in trouble. Eric tells me he has his lifesaver medallion but I'd rather not test his skills.'

'I…I'll just have water, then.' Caroline frowned—and Erin frowned right back. She turned to the punch table and handed Caroline a paper cup—empty.

'We have all the water you want, and it's purer than tank water—but it's still in the river,' she told her guest. 'I'm afraid you'll have to walk twenty yards upstream to avoid sand from the swimmers. If you're being nice, you could take a jug and bring some back—in case anyone else has the same idea.'

Caroline took one step backwards and her eyes narrowed—as if she was suspecting Erin of making fun of her. A party where everything wasn't laid on…

'I don't think I'll bother…'

'I'll get you some,' Mike said. He smiled down at Erin, his eyes dancing. 'Some party…'

'You ain't seen nothin' yet.' Erin grinned at him cheekily—and their eyes locked. The laughter in both eyes linked and held—like an invisible knot.

Shared laughter. It was a bond so strong between them that surely Caroline could feel it.

'I...I'm sorry I can't fetch the water. I can't leave the punch bowl...' Erin's voice had suddenly become a whisper and Caroline looked at her sharply.

'I don't suppose you can.' Mike's smile had faded as well. He looked uncertainly down at the colour draining from Erin's face—and then suddenly wheeled and stalked upriver.

'Michael!'

Caroline called him back sharply and he stopped. It took him seconds to turn, though. It was as if he didn't want to.

Finally he did, swivelling to face Erin and Caroline standing side by side.

'Yes?' His face was carefully expressionless.

'You forgot the jug,' Caroline said nastily. 'And do make it fast, Michael. I'm thirsty.'

Ugh...

What on earth did he see in the woman? Erin pondered the match unhappily as she doled out good humour and punch in equal measure throughout the afternoon.

Mike sure didn't look happy.

Erin caught only fleeting glimpses of him as she worked—and when she did she thought that he and his lady seemed to be the only two who weren't having a great time. They stood slightly aloof—Caroline giving clear vibes that she thought the party childish and Mike apparently unable to leave her side.

Maybe he did regret his engagement, Erin thought hopelessly. Maybe Mike had asked Caroline to marry him in panic at the thought of parenthood—and now he regretted it.

It didn't matter one whit what he regretted. Even if he were free he wouldn't marry Erin. Erin was an unsuitable bride for Mike McTavish. He'd made that abundantly clear.

Oh, for heaven's sake... Stop thinking about that and think about your guests, Erin told herself harshly. She should be making sure people were enjoying themselves.

They all were. The birthday boy was having a ball and everyone else seemed to be following suit. Only Mike and Caroline were miserable.

In fairness to Caroline there really weren't many people here she'd know well, Erin conceded—but then Caroline could at least try to be sociable. Anyone approaching her was greeted with monosyllabic replies, and Mike, at her side, was finding the going tough.

The twins were swinging from the trees and paddling in the river—but Caroline and Mike had the look of a couple who might bolt for home any minute.

Erin couldn't worry about them. She couldn't...

She couldn't think of anyone else but dratted Mike McTavish and his horrible fiancée. Bother the man. Why had he come if he meant to be so aloof?

At the end of an hour Caroline had clearly had enough. Erin, collecting empty plates, walked past them in time to hear her complaining of a headache.

'Take me home, Michael,' she was saying. 'You come back if you feel you should—but, honestly, I think you've done your duty by now. They can't expect you to stay—as if you'd enjoy something like this. Honestly, there's not even any wine.'

Erin flushed crimson and dug her nails into her palms. Instead of a rude retort, though, she forced a smile onto her lips as she turned to Caroline. She was practically sure she'd been meant to hear Caroline's crack.

'You can't go yet,' she smiled. 'Not until after the birthday cake.'

'You've had a birthday cake made?' Mike demanded, and Erin raised her eyebrows and flashed him a mock pout.

'I'm getting insults from all sides.' She sighed dramatically. 'Oh, ye of little faith. I've made it myself.'

'This I have to see.' Mike grinned and Erin bobbed a curtsey.

'Your wish is my command—sir. Just hang onto your hats.'

Then she was gone, with Mike staring after her in bemusement.

She didn't go up to the house to fetch the cake, though. Instead, Erin hiked across to the nearest tree and hauled herself up onto its lowest branches.

The band seemed to hush. Word flew round—and suddenly all the party guests were watching the slight, elfin-like figure shimmy up her tree.

The tree was a breeze to climb. The twins and many of the children present had been halfway up it—but not all the way to the top. If they had, they'd have realized that one of Erin's banners had been concealing a huge round hat box, glittering in silver foil with a huge red ribbon attached. All round the side of the box was painted the words: HAPPY BIRTHDAY, JACK! in brilliant crimson lettering. The box looked for all the world like a giant birthday cake.

A birthday box!

Erin straddled the highest branch and pulled back the cover.

The box was crammed to bursting with every berry Erin could find on the farm—strawberries, raspberries, blackcurrants, loganberries... You name it, it was squashed in there, all stirred up with sugar and a trace of orange liqueur.

And Erin had topped it with cream, whipped stiff enough to hold candles.

There was, in fact, only one large candle, buried solidly in the centre of the cream. Leaning lightly against that, though, was a sparkler tied to a thin wire cable— and above that there was another sparkler—and another and another, twisted around the flexible cable and looped in a bunch around the branch.

Erin had spent hours the day before wiring them just right, and adjusting the pulleys.

Now she lit her central candle—and let the pulleys go.

And the box-cake swung slowly, slowly down through the trees, the sparklers lighting in steady procession until the whole wonderful confection was a mass of glitter— a moving sparkling candle, fifty feet high, moving slowly down through the trees.

Jack was staring up in stunned amazement as around him people laughed and clapped and thumped him on the back and wished him more birthdays like this—just like this, they demanded.

And, high in the branches, Erin's eyes suddenly filled with tears. She wanted her father to be here so badly that it was a physical hurt.

It wasn't fair.

It was so right for her to be here. But Jack should have had his son. It wasn't fair.

She couldn't go down. Not feeling like this. Instead, Erin sat in her treetop refuge and watched the people attack the birthday box below through a mist of tears. She was homesick. She missed her parents so much it hurt.

And the man she loved was down below holding another woman's hand.

She closed her eyes, blocking out pain—and found he wasn't doing any such thing.

How Mike came up so silently she didn't know—but all of a sudden Mike's hand was on her shoulder and Erin jumped about a foot.

The last thing she'd expected here was company.

The last thing she'd expected was Mike. For heaven's sake, she was howling like a baby!

'Erin…'

Erin sniffed frantically—and found a handkerchief being placed in her hands. She took it with real gratitude and retired into its welcome depths, fighting to recover some semblance of dignity.

'You weren't supposed to come up here,' she managed, her voice muffled by the handkerchief. 'I didn't think anyone could.'

'You thought you were the only one with wings?' Mike smiled, watching her with grave, compassionate eyes. He'd swung himself to the opposite branch now, not trusting one branch with their combined weights, and was a whole eighteen inches away. There was a fifty-foot drop between them.

A world of distance.

'I've been climbing trees for a sight longer than you,' he told her. 'Anything you can do…'

'I can do better? That…that sounds like a challenge…' Erin gave a watery sniff and emerged from behind the handkerchief, looking doubtfully down at it in her hand.

'I'm not challenging you. I don't intend to go one inch higher—and, no, I don't want it back,' Mike smiled. 'You can start a collection.'

'I…I'll wash it.'

'I'd recommend it.' Still that same gentle teasing—a voice that showed Mike was seeing clearly behind the pain. 'Would you care to tell me why you're up a tree, howling, in the middle of the best party I've been to for years?'

Erin looked down. The guests were still attacking the birthday box with relish.

There were many who were concentrating on other things beside birthday cake. Her fire brigade helper had started the water pump as Erin had lit the birthday cake—just in case there were sparks—and he'd let the hose spray onto the dusty track on the far side of the river where the cattle came down to drink.

Egged on by the children to keep the pump going, he'd done so, and there was now a vast, muddy water slide down into the river—and the kids were screaming in delight as they rolled and tumbled down.

No one had eyes for the two in the tree.

'It is a good party,' Erin whispered.

'The best. You should be proud.' Mike leaned forward and took her hand. 'Now…would you like to tell me why you're crying?'

'I'm not… I never—'

'Okay. You never cry. Would you like to tell me why you're needing my handkerchief?'

There was a long silence. Erin closed her eyes and let her legs swing free. The warm wind caressed her face like a healing balm.

'It's only…' She swallowed. 'I guess I felt a bit homesick all of a sudden. My…my dad would so love to be here.'

'He'd be proud of you,' Mike said gently. 'What you're doing, Erin O'Connell, is very, very special. There's no other woman I know who'd give the gift of love so completely…'

The gift of love.

Mike was talking of what she'd done for her grandfather. He wasn't talking of what she'd given him.

The gift of love.

To be worth anything at all, a gift had to be received. And Mike didn't want what she was offering.

'I…' Erin took a deep breath. 'I'll have to go down. The punch…'

'There are three old ladies clucking over the punch like they own it.' Mike smiled. 'They love the responsibility. Like the twins and their pavlovas. You've made everyone happy, Erin O'Connell.'

'Except Caroline,' Erin whispered before she could help herself. 'Mike, you'd better go. Caroline won't like you being up here.'

She certainly wouldn't. They must be clearly visible from below, Erin realized, and what Caroline thought of her prospective husband swinging from the trees with Erin O'Connell beside him was anyone's guess.

'Caroline knows you're my friend,' Mike said firmly. 'It's…it's taking us both a while to get adjusted to each other—and each other's friends—but we'll manage.'

His voice was all of a sudden grim—the voice of a man facing a future he wasn't the least sure of.

'As long as you can be happy…' Erin whispered.

'Yeah… Well, we will be. Caroline's very sure…' Mike's voice dropped away. He looked across at Erin and swore suddenly under his breath. 'If only…'

'If only doesn't come into it,' Erin said bleakly. She swung herself from her branch and dropped to the next level. 'Does it, Mike? Like my dad. Life's tossed him an ultimatum and he has to live with it. Sometimes it seems so darned unfair—but it's life. And if Dad can keep living in the States…'

She didn't go on—but the inference was plain as day: Erin was going to have to keep living here—keep living side by side with this man as neighbour only—and it would break her heart.

'Hell…' This time there was no suppressing Mike's oath. 'Erin…'

'There's nothing to say,' Erin said bleakly. 'Please, Mike… Come down and enjoy what's left of Jack's party. Please…'

He didn't.

Mike and Erin reached the foot of the tree to find Caroline rigid with suppressed fury, holding the twins by two repulsive collars.

They'd been two of the first down the mud slide in their Sunday best—and were matted with wet mud. It was all Erin could do not to giggle.

'Why don't you let them swim and clean off?' she suggested, but Caroline treated the advice with the contempt it deserved. She ignored Erin completely and directed her wrath at Mike.

'You, climbing trees when you should have been

watching them…' Her face tightened with anger as she glared at Mike. 'Of all the… I'll never get the stains from their clothing. Michael, my headache's worse. I want you to take us home now!'

It was take her home or face full-scale war—and Mike shrugged and acquiesced.

'Okay, Caroline.' He turned and took Erin's hand. 'But it was a great party—wasn't it, twins?'

'The best party in the world,' Laura declared, and Matt nodded furiously.

'Thank you for coming.' It was a polite platitude but it was all she was capable of. Erin just wished they'd go. The pain round her heart was threatening to overwhelm her.

'I've a proposition for you, before we go,' Mike said firmly. He cast a doubtful look at Caroline's rigid face and then shrugged. 'Erin, our local horse trials are next Saturday. Dressage. The show's open nationwide and there are displays from our national champion riders. There's a lunch provided for the top riders and I can organize an invitation for you if you'd like to come.'

It was a challenge.

Get back into gear, his eyes said. Face the pain and work through it.

'I don't think…'

'Sweetheart, the lunch is for Grand Prix riders and local organizers and fund raisers,' Caroline said sweetly. 'Don't you think Erin might feel a little out of place?'

'Erin can ride…'

'Well, of course she can.' Caroline smiled. 'But I'm intermediate and if I wasn't on the social committee even *I* wouldn't be asked to lunch. These people…they really don't like outsiders.'

For 'these people' read Caroline Podger, Erin thought grimly, and she flushed and bit her lip.

'Caroline…' Mike said angrily, but Erin shook her head.

'Caroline's right. I am an outsider,' she said softly.

'Thank you for the invitation, but no, thanks. Now…if
you'll excuse me I really have to get back to our guests.'

And for that read, I really have to get away from Mike
McTavish before I cry, she thought—and I really have
to get away from Caroline Podger before I tell her what
I think of her.

'But we can't go,' the twins wailed as one, staring
longingly back at the mud slide. 'We can't.'

Erin hesitated. All she wanted was to be shot of the
lot of them—but maybe not of the twins.

No. Not of the twins.

'Mike, the twins are so filthy a little more mud won't
hurt them,' she managed. 'If I promise to look after
them, can I send them home later?'

'No!' Caroline exploded—but Mike shook his head.

'The twins shouldn't suffer because you have a headache,' he said grimly. 'I'll take you home, Caroline, but
the twins can stay. Thank you, Erin.'

His words were so harsh it was as though he was
punishing himself somehow.

'Yahoo!' the twins yelled in chorus, and Laura hugged
Erin hard, covering her with mud in the process. 'Erin,
you're the best.'

No, I'm not, Erin thought sadly as she watched Mike
and Caroline depart hand in hand. I'm the second best.

CHAPTER FOURTEEN

THE party went on until dusk, and then Erin was faced with hours of cleaning up. She worked until the last trace of the party had disappeared and the river looked as it always had in the moonlight—apart from one very muddy track marked by innumerable bottoms.

In the end hardly any of the adults had been able to resist the mud slide. They'd joined the children in taking turns and the party had ended with almost everyone in the river. Even the demure old ladies from church had twittered and yearned and finally succumbed. Erin had never seen a filthier set of guests off home, and she knew Jack O'Connell's eightieth birthday would be talked of for years.

A good party.

A great party.

So why did she feel so darned miserable?

Finally she made her way up to the house to find Jack waiting for her. She'd ordered him home hours ago. The old man was tired beyond belief, and by now she'd expected him to be fast asleep, but he was rocking contentedly on the verandah, surveying his domain with the air of a man supremely at peace.

As Erin appeared he smiled wearily up at her and motioned her to sit beside him.

'I know you're tired, girl.' He smiled. 'But it does you more good than sleep to watch the stars and think over a perfect day.'

'A perfect day?'

'Yep.' He stretched and a shadow flitted behind his eyes. 'It only wanted your dad here to make it the best.'

'Mmm…'

There was a long silence, each of them deep in their own thoughts, and then Erin reached out a hand and took Jack's.

'Grandpa, there were a couple of video cameras going full-throttle today. We'll send a copy to Dad so at least he can see what a good time we had.'

'We will.' Jack stirred from melancholy. 'Erin, there's been a phone call tonight while you were still down at the river. A lass called Wendy Reynolds.'

Wendy Reynolds. Erin frowned, trying to place the name—and then things clicked into place.

She knew Wendy. Wendy was the current Australian women's dressage champion. Erin had met her in America.

'How on earth…?'

'Wendy heard you were in Australia somewhere near here.' Jack smiled. 'She's rung twenty-three O'Connells looking for you and we're the twenty-fourth. I said you'd ring her back but it's a bit late now.'

'It is.' It was awfully close to midnight. 'Did she say what she wanted?'

'She did, as a matter of fact,' Jack said thoughtfully. 'She wants you to ride at the local dressage event next Saturday.'

'Ride…' Erin frowned. 'But she must know I can't compete. Even if I had citizenship…well…'

'It'd be unfair,' Jack said in quiet satisfaction. 'For an Olympian to be pitting herself against the local talent… No, that's not what Wendy is asking. Seems she agreed to ride exhibition—Kür routine, she said, which from what she tells me is dressage to music. You and Paddy work to music, don't you?'

'Yes. But…'

'Erin, Wendy's horse has gone lame. She'll be out of action for a month or more and they've advertised Wendy's riding as a drawcard. Proceeds from the exhibition go to riding for the disabled so she's feeling bad—

and she asked whether you and Paddy could take her place.'

'Grandpa…I can't…'

'Because you don't ride in Australia,' Jack said gently. 'Because it hurts too much.'

'I don't…'

'Now, don't think I don't understand what you're going through, Erin girl,' Jack growled. 'I know what you've given up on my account. All I'm saying…' He sighed. 'Well, Paddy's a damned fine horse, and it's a shame to retire him completely. Maybe if you did a bit of exhibition work again—met a few of your own crowd and kept your talents honed—it wouldn't seem such a harsh break from your life in the States and it wouldn't hurt as much.'

'It doesn't hurt.'

'That's not the truth,' Jack said softly. 'Is it, Erin?'

'I guess…I guess not.'

'You and Paddy make a wonderful team,' Jack told her. 'And I've never seen what you're capable of in the flesh. It'd make me proud if you rode next Saturday— and it'd make me a darned sight less guilty about keeping you here.'

'You're not keeping me.'

'I know. You want to stay. Well, prove it to me, girl, by not chopping off your talent at the knees because displaying it will make you so homesick you'll burst.' He rose to his feet, shaky with old age and fatigue. 'Think about it, Erin lass.' He smiled and stooped to kiss her on the cheek. 'Think about it. And thank you for a darned fine party. You've given me a gift more precious than life itself—just by being here. And maybe—maybe if you started riding again… Maybe that way watching Mike McTavish marry someone else might not quite break your heart.'

Erin didn't move.

She sat staring out at the stars, thoughts mingling disjointedly in her tired mind.

Grandpa knew. They were kindred spirits, she and Jack O'Connell. She might have known there was no fooling him.

And maybe he was right.

She was breaking her heart here on three levels. Firstly, missing home. Secondly, missing riding. And third…

Jack knew.

Erin bit her lip, trying to block out the thought of Mike McTavish as she came to a sensible, pragmatic decision. How hard was that?

To ride on Saturday…

Erin had thought she could give up riding at Grand Prix level without a backward glance—but she was wrong, she acknowledged, still shoving the image of Mike McTavish away. Both she and Paddy were missing riding at international standard like a physical ache. So much discipline suddenly gone…

And this was the event Mike had invited her to.

She could no sooner block out the thought of Mike McTavish than she could fly.

He'd be there. Caroline would be there.

Caroline would hate it.

What had the woman said to Mike?

'Don't you think Erin might feel a little out of place?' and, 'They really don't like outsiders.'

Erin stirred uneasily. She knew enough about dressage riders to know she'd be welcomed warmly by everyone except Caroline Podger.

She'd have to face Mike.

Mike…

And Erin found herself taking a deep breath and squaring her shoulders.

Mike McTavish thought she was so unsuitable—because she wasn't sophisticated and domesticated. He'd seen her at her worst. Neck-deep in soap suds with cream puffs and toffee spread liberally around under water level. Climbing trees. Heaving hay in her filthy work clothes. Never once had he seen her as she could be.

In her wardrobe were clothes Erin had never worn in this country. She'd thought she never could—but at the last moment she'd decided she couldn't bear to leave them. She'd brought them to Australia 'just in case'.

Maybe she'd known she'd break her resolution.

Jack's dog stirred at Erin's feet, thumped her tail on the verandah boards and rose to look at Erin with large, questioning eyes. It was as if the old dog sensed her indecision.

'Okay, Sadie.' Erin caressed the labrador's golden ears and Sadie practically purred with pleasure. 'Want a walk to the stables? Let's go and ask Paddy what he thinks I should do.'

There was never any doubting what Paddy thought.

Erin spent much of the next week going through her routines with Paddy, and the old horse's mood lifted perceptibly.

He'd done this for years. Paddy was arguably the best dressage horse in the world—and even though his limbs were beginning to stiffen with age, this was the work he loved.

Erin played her Kür routine tapes up high as they practised and her lovely old horse seemed to shake the stiffness from his knees and lift his head with pride.

In the days that followed Paddy had never worked better. It was as if he intended showing off his skills to all concerned.

Erin, however, didn't permit him to show off to anyone but her. Absurdly self-conscious, Erin took Paddy out to practise behind the haystack when the twins weren't around—and Jack wasn't permitted near.

'I want you to see us on Saturday for the first time,' Erin told him firmly. 'You've bullied me into this. Now we'll do it my way.'

She had to get it right.

Jack was so proud. She had to get it right for Jack's sake.

Not only that. She had to get it right because Mike McTavish would be watching.

They were five long days but finally they ended.

Erin spent early Saturday morning feeling exactly the same as the day she'd ridden for Olympic silver.

Scared stiff.

This is crazy, she told herself over and over again as the time to leave for the showgrounds grew nearer. She and Jack had been up since dawn preparing Paddy. Her beautiful horse now stood in resplendent glory, his glossy mane and forelock plaited with care and his tail also plaited for the first few inches to make the silken tresses stand out. Now his body was a long, gleaming line of absolute elegance.

Paddy had been shampooed, conditioned and groomed until he gleamed like black diamonds in the morning sun. Erin stood back to admire him and thought back to the first time she'd seen him—a failure of a steeple-chaser with a tendency to buck—destined for the knacker's yard. Erin's father had looked over him with a horseman's eye and seen what was beneath the uncared-for exterior, and he and Erin had bought him on the spot.

Even as old as he was, Paddy was worth diamonds now. More than that, Erin thought affectionately, letting him nuzzle her neck.

Paddy was so pleased this was happening. His mighty frame seemed tense and his eyes were alert and interested. This wasn't the stance of an ageing, retired horse. This was the stance of a horse preparing to meet his adoring public.

'And if they don't adore you, I'll eat my hat,' Erin declared as she loaded him into her shabby trailer. 'Hey, Paddy, the way you look you should be in a chauffeur-driven limousine.'

Not so Erin.

She'd groomed her hair into a sleek knot in honour of the day, but the rest of her gear was spread carefully in the back of the truck. She wore her normal jeans and a checked, short-sleeved shirt. Erin didn't intend to strut her stuff until it was time.

'Okay, Grandpa?' With Paddy loaded she turned to Jack, a trace of uncertainty in her eyes. 'Ready?'

'Sure am.' Jack hauled himself into the passenger side of Erin's truck and gazed ahead with contentment. 'Let's go. Let's knock 'em dead, Erin, girl.'

The first people Erin saw as they pulled into the show-ground were the twins. They spotted Erin's truck from a distance and came haring over the grass at breakneck speed.

'What are you doing here, Erin? Why did you bring Paddy? Are you going to ride?' They stopped, breathless with excitement, and waited.

'I thought I might.' Erin hesitated as she climbed down from the truck—and then looked behind them to where Mike and Caroline were following. Together. Hand in hand, in fact.

It was all Erin could do not to climb back into the truck and bolt for cover. Somehow, though, she managed to stay where she was and school her expression into something approaching a smile of greeting.

She couldn't deny these two were well matched, she thought bitterly as she watched them walk slowly over the grass towards her. They were indeed a handsome couple. Mike was wearing good, casual trousers with a quality linen open-necked shirt. His thick hair was tousled with the light wind and he was laughing at something Caroline was saying. His eyes were creased in the sunlight—with an expression in them that Erin knew and loved so much...

She didn't have one snowball's chance in a bushfire here, she thought bitterly. Mike McTavish was marrying the girl beside him in a few short weeks—and Caroline Podger was gorgeous.

Caroline was in full dressage gear. She was all in black and white, with top boots clinging to her slim calves and shining with expensive gloss, figure-hugging breeches and tail coat moulding her figure to perfection and the stock at her throat tied with just the right attention to understated elegance.

In her hand she carried a whip.

Erin frowned at the sight of it, temporarily diverted from those linked hands. Caroline's expensive outfit suggested she was almost Grand Prix level—and she'd said she was intermediate—but no dressage rider at that level should compete using a whip.

'Erin…' Mike was smiling in welcome. He let Caroline's hand drop and reached to take Erin's in greeting.

Drat the man. Didn't he know what his touching her did to her insides? Somehow Erin let her hand lie in his for a moment—and then pulled back, as if burned.

'I'm glad you decided to come,' Mike said warmly. He looked doubtfully up at the trailer. 'Are you competing?'

'No,' Erin said shortly, turning to Caroline. 'Hello.'

She really had tried to make her voice warm—but there was no glimmer of warmth in Caroline's look.

'If you're thinking of competing you'll have to borrow some gear,' Caroline said brusquely. 'This club has standards…'

'I've told you.' Erin forced herself to smile. 'I'm not competing.'

'Then why did you bring your horse?'

'He felt like a picnic,' Erin snapped—and then sighed and smiled again. 'I'm sorry. I just…'

'It doesn't matter.' Caroline's eyes flashed fire. 'I can't stand round talking. I'm due to ride in ten minutes.'

'Intermediate, I think you said?' Erin's eyes fell to the whip in Caroline's hand and Caroline followed her gaze.

'Oh, I don't use this in the arena,' she said carelessly, reaching up to give Mike a formal kiss on the cheek before departing. 'The blasted horse has to know who's boss before he gets in front of the judges, though. The last time I rode in competition he blew up and was all over the place.'

Blew up... The equestrian term for a horse playing up on his rider.

I'd blow up too if I had Caroline Podger on my back, Erin thought grimly.

Caroline strode away—and Erin wasn't the only one who sighed in relief. The twins' combined grin as they watched her go was wider than their combined faces.

'Come and watch the riding with us,' Mike suggested, his gaze following Caroline as she disappeared into the crowd. Finally her smart top hat disappeared completely and he turned his attention back to Erin. 'We have seats reserved in the grandstand.'

His eyes were suddenly uncertain—as though he wasn't at all sure he wanted to sit next to Erin for the next couple of hours—and Erin shook her head.

Ditto. She sure as heck didn't want to sit next to Mike McTavish. Besides, she had things to do.

'Grandpa would love a seat,' she demurred softly. 'If you could look after him, I'd be grateful. But I...I'd just prefer to watch by myself. And I...' She met his questioning eyes. 'I might browse among the officials. See if there's anyone I know.'

'Why did you bring Paddy?' Mike asked her directly, his look thoughtful now. His gaze rested squarely on Erin's carefully knotted hair.

'I told you,' Erin said blithely. 'He wanted to come for a picnic.' And she departed swiftly before any more awkward questions came her way.

Erin spent the next two hours avoiding McTavishes and Caroline, being greeted with real pleasure by the organ-

izing committee and gearing herself to go out and face
an audience for the first time in close to a year.

She dressed in the public ladies' dressing room, scared
all the time that Caroline would walk in. Caroline didn't,
for which Erin was profoundly thankful. She'd had
enough of the woman's spite.

It was as if Caroline sensed how Erin felt about Mike.
As if she knew.

'Well, I'm no threat to you, lady,' Erin told the absent
Caroline bitterly, under her breath. She turned to face
the mirror and sighed. 'No threat at all.'

Like Caroline, Erin also wore standard dressage
gear—all black and white with close-fitting breeches and
jacket—but not quite the quality that Caroline wore.

It wasn't necessary to spend a fortune on gear, Erin
thought grimly. A rider should look almost part of her
horse. Caroline was dressed so all eyes would stay on
her. Erin, on the other hand, dressed carefully so horse
and rider would merge as one.

Erin stared at herself for a long moment, trying to see
herself as Mike McTavish would see her.

She wasn't a patch on Caroline. Not even close.
Smaller and plainer and…and just plain mousier, she
decided sadly.

Well, at least she didn't carry a whip in her hand.
Literally or metaphorically.

Erin lifted her top hat, pinned it demurely to her hair
and gave herself one last, long disillusioned look.

And then it was time to join Paddy.

If Erin was nervous, Paddy would have none of it.

The old horse greeted her with unquestionable delight,
nibbling her top hat as if to say, Welcome back.

'Yeah, well, let's get on with it,' Erin said. She fixed
his saddle cloth and saddle, her United States colours
proudly blazing, then swung easily up onto his high
back. They walked a few times round the mounting yard,
taking each other's measure. Once upon a time Erin had

ridden Paddy for an hour or more before competing in order to settle him, but now Paddy seemed more settled than Erin.

Finally the morning competition ended. Caroline, Erin was interested to hear, was nowhere among those placed.

Maybe her horse had blown up again.

Then the lady in charge of the music tapes signalled Erin. Erin nodded. An announcement came over the loudspeaker.

'Ladies and gentlemen, today we're delighted to have with us Miss Erin O'Connell, an Olympic silver med-allist and World Cup finalist all the way from the United States, riding Newlyn Black Magic...'

There was more of the same. Erin didn't listen. Nei-ther did Paddy. They were both firming, tightening, fo-cusing every fibre of their combined being, listening for the first bar of Erin's medley to announce the start of their routine.

To start their magic.

And it was magic.

If Erin had ridden this way at the Olympics the gold would have been theirs. Paddy might well be stiffening in old age, but today it was as if he was putting his heart and soul into performing for a beloved public—and Erin didn't let him down.

Newlyn Black Magic—otherwise known as Paddy. Erin's wonder horse. Best horse in the world.

Paddy could feel the music. It wasn't Erin's control holding him to tempo. The big horse practically danced on his feet, light and long and high. He didn't trot. He floated through the routine. And Erin's heart swelled with love and pride.

His passage still had the power to take her breath away. Erin sat high on her wonderful horse and it was like floating on magic. Paddy moved into piaffe and she heard gasps from the crowd. This was riding at its most exquisite.

Erin's gloved hands didn't move. They didn't need to.

They knew each other so well, this horse and this girl, that they anticipated each other's wishes, and Erin could never tell who was calling the shots when it cáme to such a finely tuned performance.

Paddy's hooves never missed a beat. He pirouetted on a sixpence. And beyond the music there was now an absolute, wondrous hush from the crowd.

This crowd was seeing something special—and they knew it. Not even someone who didn't know one end of a horse from another could fail to be moved by this performance.

This was a once-in-a-lifetime experience. The coming together of perfect horse, perfect rider and perfect moment.

And when it was over, and Erin had saluted the judges, who'd been able, for once, to stop dictating to their pencillers and just enjoy, Erin rode out of the arena with tears in her eyes. She slid down from Paddy's back and hugged him so hard the old horse nuzzled her in concern.

'Oh, Paddy… Oh, you wonder horse. Oh, Paddy…'

And then she was surrounded by a throng of admirers, and Paddy was being taken from her by a beaming Jack and carefully removed before the fuss became too much for him. And the twins were launching themselves at her through the crowd.

'Erin, you were beautiful. And Paddy was magic. They said his name was Magic. You never told us he could dance…'

And Mike was there beside her, his eyes warm and wondering. He took her hand and held it.

Erin looked up at this man she loved so much, her eyes still bright with tears—and found she couldn't speak.

'Erin…'

He got no further. Mike, too, had lost his voice. The buzz around them fell to nothing. There was only a man and woman, searching each other's eyes and seeing immutable truth.

Seeing that what was between them was something so precious it had to be faced. It should be treated as something as precious as life itself.

But it couldn't be faced here. Not now.

'Michael!'

The word was practically a screech, coming from nowhere. Somehow…somehow Erin managed to pull her hand from Mike's hold—and somehow she managed to turn and face a vengeful Caroline Podger.

It was too late, of course. Caroline had seen the linked hands—and seen the look between Mike and Erin. She knew what was between them. She stood rigid before Erin, mortification and fury emanating in almost tangible waves.

'You bitch!' she said clearly, and the talk and laughter and congratulations died instantly to deathly silence.

'I—I beg your pardon?' Erin whispered faintly, and looked helplessly up at Mike.

'Caroline! What—?'

Mike's exclamation got no further. Caroline Podger was white with humiliated rage—way beyond control—and nothing Mike could say or do was powerful enough to block her tirade. Someone would have had to gag her and carry her away kicking and scratching to silence this level of fury.

'You did this today just to show me up,' Caroline hissed at Erin, ignoring Mike completely. 'You've made me a laughing stock. Set me up.'

'I didn't…'

Caroline wasn't listening.

'You don't belong here,' she spat. 'You never have and you never will. Your father cleared out of this district years ago, and we're well shot of him, so why don't you clear out, too? And if you don't, then those of us who control things around here—those of us with real social clout—will just have to make you.'

And then, before anyone realized what the woman
intended—before anyone even suspected she was capable of such an act—Caroline's hand raised, with the
whip firmly clenched between her fingers. It hung mo-
mentarily still—and then, as Mike launched himself forward with a savage oath, the whip slashed down through
the air.

Mike was too late to stop its swing. The thong slashed
hard across Erin's cheek.

It was Mike who grabbed Caroline before she could
strike again.

While everyone else was still frozen with shock it was
Mike who imprisoned Caroline's hand, even as it raised
again for another blow, wrenching the whip from her
fingers and hauling his fiancée roughly away from the
gaping crowd.

There was another long moment of appalled silence
as Mike hauled Caroline somewhere blessedly out of
sight.

And then it was up to others—members of an appalled
committee—to hustle Erin unprotestingly into the dressing room, to stem the blood from the graze on Erin's
cheek and fetch the doctor to ensure she didn't need a
stitch. It was up to others—so many people—to assure
her they would never have had this happen for the
world. To assure her they were appalled…appalled…
appalled…

So was Erin.

She sat numb, trying to come to terms with the naked
hate she'd seen in Caroline's eyes.

What had she done to deserve such hatred? Nothing,
she told herself bleakly. Caroline had hated Erin from
first setting eyes on her.

And Mike was marrying Caroline. Caroline Podger
had it all.

Or maybe she didn't.

Maybe Caroline had seen what was between Erin and
Mike. Even though Mike was rejecting Erin's love,

maybe Caroline knew that Erin would so joyously take her place…

Maybe…maybe she couldn't stay here, Erin thought bleakly. Maybe Erin couldn't stand by and watch the man she loved marry such a woman. Maybe Caroline was right. Maybe she should go home.

Leave Grandpa?

The world spun dizzily around her.

'Erin…'

Erin had been hustled into the women's dressing room. There were women clucking all around, mortified beyond belief that such an honoured guest should be so treated, and Erin almost didn't hear the small, scared voice from the doorway.

She did, though.

Laura.

Erin looked up through the crowd of people and met the child's terrified eyes, and it was suddenly too much to bear. That Caroline be mother to this child… She stood, took two tentative steps towards Laura and then was cradling the frightened child to her—holding her so tightly it was as if she needed comfort as much as Laura.

'Hush, Laura. You're not to cry. You're not.' Erin made a huge effort to make herself smile. 'See…I'm fine. There's just a spot of sticking plaster on my face and a small graze underneath.'

'She shouldn't have hit you. She shouldn't.'

'No.' Around them the ladies of the organizing committee had fallen back, unsure of what was happening but decent enough not to interfere in what they sensed was important. 'Caroline shouldn't have hit me, Laura,' Erin agreed.

'But…' She took a deep breath. 'Laura, I should have told your aunt Caroline that I was riding today. Maybe…' She winced. 'Laura, if you're doing something and you're the best—the absolute best at it and everyone tells you how wonderful you are—and then someone comes along and suddenly they're miles better than you, I guess for a moment you'd be pretty shocked—and maybe angry, too.'

'Not angry enough to hit. And Caroline's not the best,' Laura whispered. 'She hits her poor horse all the time and when she was riding Grandpa said she hauled her horse so hard it spent its time below the bit. And that her hands were all over the place. Whatever that means,' she added honestly.

'I'll explain that to you next lesson,' Erin promised gently. 'But meanwhile… Laura, maybe when Caroline's thought about it she'll be sorry and a bit ashamed of what she's done—and maybe we can be forgiving and forget what's happened. I mean, it's not as if I'm really hurt, now, is it?'

Laura drew back and inspected Erin's sticking plaster with something less than horror. Something approaching a ghoulish six-year-old's interest.

'Is it still bleeding underneath?'

'No.'

'Okay, then.' Finally satisfied, Laura wriggled free from Erin's grasp. 'I'll tell Mike and Matthew. They can't come in here because it's the ladies' dressing room, so I was the only one allowed in. And Mike said I had to be quick because we have to take *Caroline* home.' Her small mouth voiced the name as something distasteful. 'Not to our place, Mike said, but to her place. But Matt and me have decided we're not going to talk to her. Not once. Not ever, ever again, and we're not going to do what she says and we're not living with her. Me and Matt have decided absolutely. Not ever!'

She looked up at Erin's bandaged face and managed a small, shy smile. 'But apart from that, if you tell us we have to, I suppose we can be…we can be forgiving…'

CHAPTER FIFTEEN

Jack wasn't in the least forgiving.

He swore all the way home and he swore for the rest of the day.

'She should be horsewhipped herself, that girl. Put in the stocks and made a public spectacle. She thinks she's so far above the likes of us she doesn't have to accord us common human decency. You could sue her for millions, Erin.'

'Could I? Compensation for pain and suffering from one scratched face?' Erin gave a shaky laugh as she combed out Paddy's mane and settled him for the night. 'Maybe I asked for it, Grandpa. I should have told her what I'd done in the past.'

'She hardly gave you the opportunity,' Jack snapped. 'I'm off to bed now, girl, but I doubt if I'll sleep. I'll lie there and think about tarring and feathering...or maybe something a little more permanent. Maybe something like boiling oil...'

He went off muttering to himself and Erin was left alone with Paddy.

There'd been no word from the McTavishes. Nothing. The committee had insisted Erin stay on for lunch and they would have been mortified if she'd refused—and then she'd found herself acting as guest judge for the afternoon's competition. Still, she'd been home for three hours now. Time enough for Mike to ring and check she was okay.

If he cared...

Silence.

'So what are you expecting?' Erin muttered savagely

into Paddy's ear. 'An apology from Caroline? Fat chance!'

She walked slowly back to the house and settled herself on the verandah. Sleep was impossible, even if it could include dreams of boiling oil. She sat and watched the stars and her mind was numb and blank—and so unhappy that she felt like crying.

The telephone stirred her out of her reverie.

Erin started—and then glanced at her watch. Eleven o'clock. Far too late for normal social chat.

Maybe it was her parents. With the time difference between here and the States they sometimes rang at odd hours. Erin walked into the house with a sinking heart. How was she going to sound cheerful if it was her family, for heaven's sake? They knew her so well!

It wasn't her family.

It was Mike, and the moment Erin heard his voice she knew he was in trouble.

'Erin, are the twins with you?' It was a voice Erin hardly recognized—harsh, curt and fearful.

'No.' Mike had her full attention. Indulgent self-pity was thrust firmly aside as she focused on his need.

'They've gone.'

'What do you mean, ''gone''?' Erin whispered, a cold, empty feeling starting in the pit of her stomach and spreading outward. Her hand clenched on the receiver so hard it hurt.

'They've run away again. I put them to bed at eight and Dan's been here watching television while...while I went over to Caroline's...and when I came back and checked their beds were empty. Cold. Dan's been caught up in a movie. They could have been gone for an hour or more.'

Erin licked suddenly dry lips.

'Did they—did they take their suitcase?' She cringed inwardly. The thought of the children trudging along dark roads and around blind corners was almost unbearable.

'No. But—' Mike broke off on a harsh exclamation. 'Maybe they just went without packing. They were so upset. Erin, Dan and I have searched the house and sheds and they're not here. We're sure. Now we have to check the roads.'

Mike was seeing what Erin was seeing, she thought in horror. He was seeing two tiny figures—and a car coming fast round a blind bend.

'They wouldn't try to go home to Sydney any more,' she whispered. 'They know they can't.'

'I don't know what they'd do,' Mike told her, despair and weariness etched in his words. 'I should have stayed. I should have talked to them instead of seeing Caroline.' There was a moment's silence as though Mike was fighting for control. 'Erin, I have to go. I've rung the police from Hamilton but it'll be half an hour before they get here. Dan's searching the roads north and I'm going south. Could you…' His voice hoarsened. 'Erin, are you okay to…?'

'I'm fine,' Erin managed. 'Just tell me what you want me to do.'

'Could you check the river? They loved it so much— where you had your party. I… It occurred to me they might head there.'

Of course it had.

To think of worst-case scenarios first and work backwards was every parent's gut reaction—and Mike McTavish had come a long way towards absolute parenthood since the twins had been thrust on him four months ago. Most dangerous was the road but coming a close second was the river.

'I'm on my way,' Erin whispered. She wasn't far behind Mike in the imagined horror stakes either.

'Erin, I've rung Mrs Brown. She's coming over to…to be here if they come back…and to man the phone. There's a radio in the car and she'll pass on any messages.'

'Okay, Mike.' Erin took a deep breath. 'Off you go, then—and find them.'

'Bless you.'

And he was gone.

They weren't at the river.

Erin took the truck down, bumping over the rabbit-holed paddocks and the newly mown stubble, her head-lights on full beam as she searched for two little runaways.

The river was as deserted as it always had been, with the exception of the night of the party. And the time with Mike.

The water was a dark, mysterious ribbon in the moonlight, running cool and deep.

Erin stood on the bank and forced her frightened mind to think as she strained to search each shadow. Each clump of bushes.

Surely the children wouldn't be here? Why would they come? In the daylight this place looked lovely but at night, to two frightened children, it would appear just plain scary.

Mike had been frightened they'd come here and fall in. His reasoning might well have been logical if it was hot and sunlit and tempting.

Now…

There was no way they'd be here, Erin decided flatly. Now they'd either be trying to get to Sydney again—or looking for somewhere to hide.

And all of a sudden Erin knew where.

She heard a small child's voice in the back of her head, heard almost subconsciously weeks ago but now remembered clear as day.

'What a great place for a cubbyhouse. You could almost live up here. We don't get this at our place, do we, Matt? 'Cos Mike puts his hay into big rolls.'

The haystacks.

The two giant haystacks back near the house.

Maybe…

The more Erin thought about it the more it seemed possible. She'd made it very clear to the children that Sydney was out of the question. Their parents' home wasn't an option.

And tonight… Tonight they were upset and scared about a future they didn't understand—with an aunt who scared the life out of them—and they knew that probably there was little choice for them in their future.

They were running—but around here Jack's farm was one of the few places they'd know how to reach. They knew there wouldn't be frightening dogs here and they knew the way over the paddocks to the haystacks blindfold.

'So please…' Erin whispered silently as she stumbled back over the riverbank and back into the truck.

'Please…'

The first haystack was clear of absolutely everything except for the farm cat, placidly preparing to give birth to her kittens. She squirmed round Erin's legs as if she'd quite like a midwife—but Erin had time only for a perfunctory pat and good wishes before scrambling down one pile of hay and up another.

Please… Please…

And magically—miraculously—her prayers were answered. Right in the centre of the top of the second haystack were two fair heads and two little bodies entwined, fast asleep in the moonlight on a soft bed of hay. They were huddled so close Erin had to bend over them to make sure there were two and not one.

Her relief was so intense she thought she'd cry.

For two long moments Erin stood there, letting relief wash over her in waves, and then she laid a hand on Matt's bony little shoulder to wake him.

He didn't stir—and, for the life of her, Erin couldn't shake harder.

Instead, she turned and scrambled down the hay faster

than she'd ever scrambled in her life—and flew to the house to telephone Mike McTavish.

Erin didn't wake Jack. Her grandfather had enjoyed a huge day and it was too late to wake him for something that was no longer an emergency.

Instead she left a note on the kitchen table in case he woke and worried—and then she gathered armloads of blankets and pillows and hauled her bundle over the yard and up to the top of the haystack.

The children hadn't stirred.

Soon they would, she knew. Hay was a prickly business at the best of times, and once the edge of exhaustion had passed they'd stir with a grass rash down their face and arms.

So Erin broke open a hay bale, tossing it into delicious softness, and spread a blanket over the mound. Then, very gently, she lifted the children onto the soft wool and covered them with yet another blanket.

Matt's eyes opened for a millisecond as she lifted him, but as he saw who was doing the lifting he smiled almost in his sleep and drifted back to his dreams. Laura slept on regardless.

Erin stood looking down at the pair of them, her heart doing strange things within her breast.

Something had to be arranged. If Mike McTavish still insisted on marrying that…that…

Words failed her as she thought of Caroline Podger but the feeling stayed the same. If Mike was still intent on marrying her then maybe the twins could base themselves here. Maybe she could keep the twins.

Crazy thought. Mike loved these two and they were his brother's children. Mike wouldn't have a bar of it.

Maybe he wouldn't have a choice. In marrying Caroline, how would Mike be able to stop these two making periodic escape bids? She'd do the same herself if she were six years old and Caroline Podger was playing mother.

Mike had been ten miles north when she'd called Mrs

Brown and asked her to relay the twins' whereabouts. It'd take a while for him to get here.

Meanwhile, Erin broke open another hay bale and spread blankets over it for herself, tossed on some pillows and then settled down on her makeshift bed to wait.

She didn't want Mike to take the children home tonight, she decided. She wanted to keep them here with her. If Erin had her way, she'd let them have their sleep out here and then go home in the morning—after a night of adventure.

This way would be much less chastening than being carried home in the small hours like two fugitives.

If Mike would agree.

Erin had only to wait for him, and waiting had never been so hard in all her life.

And finally Mike came.

Erin heard the truck and stirred uneasily on her mound of hay. One half of her wanted to lie here waiting—and the other wanted to run. The cowardly part of her didn't want to face Mike McTavish.

She didn't have a choice. She had to face him.

A strong flashlight cut the velvet darkness, paling the moonlight to insignificance, and then Mike was up and over the top of the piled hay, gazing incredulously from Erin to the sleeping twins.

'Good grief...' His voice was blank with astonishment. He played the torchlight over each sleeping twin, assuring himself that all was well, and then turned to gaze down at Erin.

'How on earth...?'

'Turn the torch off, Mike,' she said gently. 'You'll wake them.'

'You found them here? How did you know...?'

'I guessed they might come,' Erin told him. She looked up and saw the traces of anxiety still lingering on his face. 'I thought... They really have nowhere else to run.'

'Except to you.' Mike turned to look back down at each sleeping twin. 'They ran to you.'

'They ran to our hayshed.' There was pain in Mike's voice and Erin heard it. It was the pain of someone who loved these children—and had discovered how deeply it hurt when they ran to someone else. 'It's hardly the same as coming to me.'

'It is.' Mike stood looking down for one long moment at the sleeping faces of his tiny niece and nephew—and then clicked off the torch. It was as if he didn't want Erin to see the expressions playing across his face. As if he didn't want her to see the pain.

Silence.

The silence stretched out for ever. Two minutes. Three…

The whole world held its breath.

And finally Mike lowered himself onto the rug Erin was seated on and turned to face her, his face shadowed in the faint traces of moonlight.

'Thank you,' he said heavily. 'Thank you, Erin…'

'It was nothing.'

The world was still waiting.

'Did you bring this bedding here?' Mike asked, and it was as if he was somehow filling in time. Trying to figure out something that had nothing to do with bedding.

'We don't always have quilts left lying in the hay ready for wandering orphans,' Erin teased gently. 'I thought…I thought I'd sleep here too. If it's okay with you. This way the twins can sleep until morning. This way it'll end up being an adventure—instead of something frightening.'

'You do understand,' Mike said wonderingly, and he moved closer to the woman on the blanket, kneeling before her on the soft rug and tracing the line of sticking plaster along her cheek. He shook his head as though shaking off a fog. 'You know what it's like for them. Erin…'

She couldn't bear it. She couldn't bear him to touch her. 'No. Please, Mike...' Erin took his hand between her fingers and lifted it away from her face. 'Don't. Please...'

'Don't touch?'

'No.'

'Why not?' Mike imprisoned the slight fingers that were trying to remove his hand and he held them fast. 'Why not, Erin?'

'You...you know why not.'

'If it's because I'm engaged to Caroline, then I'm here to tell you that our engagement is officially at an end.' He shook his head as though shaking off a bad dream. 'As of tonight, Erin, Caroline and I are finished. In fact, we never ever began—only I was too blind to see that at the start, and too cowardly at the end.'

'Mike...what...?'

Erin was trying desperately to say, What do you mean? but the words stuck fast in her throat. She couldn't speak for the life of her.

'Erin, I've known Caroline for years,' Mike told her gently. 'With me she's always seemed pleasant, competent, caring. When the twins arrived—well, I'll admit I panicked. I'd never met a woman who I thought I wanted to marry and I was beginning to think I never could. And Caroline... Well, Caroline was handy and available and everything I thought I wanted. Only I was filling a job description. Not looking for...not looking for love. I didn't think I was capable of loving. Until I started loving the twins so much it hurt,' he added softly. 'And then...and then I started loving you.'

Erin stared up at him, mute. She couldn't have spoken if she had wished to. Only her eyes asked questions, eyes huge in the dim light and waiting for pain.

'Erin, Caroline and I arranged to marry almost as a business proposition,' Mike went on, his voice almost down to a whisper. The twins were so fast asleep nothing could disturb them, but the haystack was such a place

of peace that loud talk seemed almost irreligious. 'We
didn't love each other and we knew that. We talked
about it—and we agreed we could make a marriage
work. She… Well, Caroline was increasingly unhappy
living with her parents but she didn't wish to leave the
district, and I…well, you know my reasons. It seemed
so damned sensible.'

Mike was still holding her hand. His fingers played
with hers and he looked down at their intertwined link-
ing, his face tight and strained.

The last effects of the flashlight had faded from Erin's
eyes so she was accustomed again to the moonlight. She
could see his face quite clearly.

He didn't look at hers. He still watched only their
linked hands.

'And then,' Mike said gently, 'then, against all odds,
I fell in love with one totally unsuitable lady. One chit
of a girl who admitted the first time I really talked to
her that she was totally unsuited to being what I thought
I wanted in a wife. A part-woman, part-child who came
near my house and created chaos. Who turned my niece
and nephew into grubby ragamuffins. And who brought
such joy into our lives that the chaos was wonderful,
and I knew…I knew I'd made the biggest mistake of
my life in asking Caroline to marry me.'

'But…' Deep inside a tiny spark of hope was beginning to flame and spread. A tiny prayer was starting to
build. Or maybe it was a prayer so vast it took Erin's
breath away.

'I knew weeks ago,' Mike admitted. He did look at
her then, releasing her hands and cupping her face between strong fingers to force her eyes to meet his. 'I
knew I was in love. Madly, stupidly, crazily in love. But
still…' He swore softly and shook his head.

'I'd gone too far,' he told her. 'I'd promised Caroline
we'd marry, and I knew—or I thought I knew—that
Caroline could make the twins a good mother. Even
when I hated it—hated what she was doing. Like my

blasted birthday party, when she invited everyone she thought was suitable and I didn't have a friend there… But I still thought she was a sensible choice—and I didn't have the right to deprive the twins of a sensible parent. And, on top of that, I thought Caroline was my friend. I couldn't hurt or humiliate her.'

'I understand,' Erin whispered into the lovely, warming dark. The whole night was starting to seem her friend. Bring on your violins and nightingales, she thought dazedly. Things can't get any better than this. 'I—I see.'

'You see everything, my beautiful Erin,' Mike said tenderly. 'You see. You understand. You take the twins to your heart and you love them as your own. You leave your country and your parents and the riding you love to come halfway across the world—because you love your grandfather so much you can't bear to have him face old age alone. And you… Erin, you said you loved me. You offered me the most precious gift of all—and I had to turn it down. Until tonight…'

'Until tonight?' Erin was almost afraid to breathe. Almost afraid to let herself believe what was happening. She didn't have to wish for violins and nightingales. They were all around her.

Mike's finger once again touched her face, tracing the line of sticking plaster. 'Today Caroline showed me what she was capable of,' Mike said grimly. 'People have said… Friends have said… They've told me Caroline can be vicious but I'd never seen it. I thought I knew her so well. Caroline's father has a bad reputation, and I thought that alone was enough to make people judge her. I was stupid.'

'She just…' Erin took a deep breath. Suddenly she was finding it possible to feel deeply sorry for Caroline. 'Mike, I should have told her the standard I rode to. And maybe…maybe she sensed what was between us.'

'Is that an excuse for whipping someone in public?' Mike demanded. 'For making a public spectacle of both

herself and you? For hurting you?' He shook his head.
'There's no excuse at all for Caroline's behaviour. None.
I took her home—I was so angry I couldn't speak to
her—and then tonight I went across and told her our
engagement was at an end.'

Mike sighed and touched Erin's bandage yet again.
'Caroline screamed at me like a fishwife,' he told her.
'And I've never been more grateful for a cut face in all
my life. Her anger… Erin, her anger had nothing to do
with how she felt about me. It was all to do with
wounded pride, and her family's need for my money. I
hadn't seen…I hadn't clearly seen her motives for
marrying me until tonight. One cut face released me
from a lifetime commitment. It released me from the
biggest mistake of my life. But, Erin, I'm so sorry…'

'Sorry?'

'That my release came through Caroline hurting you.
And I'm so sorry she humiliated you…'

'She didn't humiliate me,' Erin said gently. 'In fact,
she's probably done me the world's biggest favour. I
now have so many friends in this district I can't count
them. So many riders came up and apologized for
Caroline's behaviour—and made real overtures of
friendship. I don't think…I don't think I ever need to be
lonely here again.'

There was a long moment of stillness.

'Does that mean…?' Mike said softly. 'Does that
mean you won't need us so much? Me…me and the
twins?'

Somewhere out in the moonlit paddocks a curlew was
calling for its mate. Its call was sweeter than any night-
ingale. The high, bright call was like an arrow in Erin's
heart, bursting it open. Instead of pain, though, instead
of pain Erin's heart was flowering like a thousand fabulous blooms.

'I think…I think I'll always need you…' she whispered.

'You mean…you think you'll need the twins.'

'I mean you.' Erin lifted her hand and touched his lips with her finger, tracing the sweetness of him. 'I've loved you since I was fourteen years old, Mike McTavish. I've never stopped loving you—not for a moment—and there's no way I'm stopping now. Not now. Not ever.'

'You mean that?'

'Absolutely.'

Mike's hand came up to imprison her finger. He sat looking down at her small, trembling hand for a long, long moment, and then, very slowly, very tenderly, Mike McTavish took Erin O'Connell in his arms.

'I love you, Erin O'Connell,' he whispered into her hair. 'If I didn't fall in love with you when you were fourteen it was only because I was a blind fool. I couldn't see...I couldn't see you had a heart as big as the land you'd come from. Erin... Erin O'Connell. My own sweet love.'

And then there was no room for words. No space.

There was no space because Mike was tilting her chin, pushing her face up to meet his. There was no space because Erin was being kissed with passion and wonder and love—and she was kissing Mike McTavish back with every trace of love in her heart.

It was right. Mike's body seemed as one with hers. Two hearts beating as one. She couldn't tell where this man's love ended and hers began. Erin's lips opened to welcome him, searching him for his taste, exploring his very being and yet knowing him already. Her hands slipped under his shirt, wanting him closer—closer— glorying in the feeling of his naked skin beneath his shirt and the sheer male hardness of his chest.

This man was her soul mate. Her life. Her heart.

And, when Mike lifted her blouse and his hands cupped the round swell of her breasts with hands that were as reverent as they were loving, she could have wept for joy. There was no inhibition left in her. She had given her heart so completely she felt as if they were already man and wife. One. Erin was sobbing, laughing and loving all in one—caressed in her cocoon of wool and hay and embraced absolutely in the arms of the man she loved—and the world was so perfect she could have burst.

Her Mike…

Her love…

But then, suddenly, Mike was pulling away from her, holding her at arm's length with a face tender and yet gravely questioning—searching her eyes in the dim light.

'Erin…'

'L-love…?' Erin's voice was a frightened whisper. She couldn't bear it if he stopped wanting her. She wanted him so much. She wanted to be held for the rest of her life.

'Erin, if I…' Mike's voice was husky with unspent passion—dark with desire. 'Erin, if I…if I hold you much longer… Love, if this goes much further I won't answer for the consequences.'

And Erin closed her eyes on the end of an answered prayer. She chuckled then, a rich, delicious chuckle that was a release from ten long years of aching. Ten long years of desire. Slowly her eyes opened once again. Her hands came around Mike's waist and she pulled him back down with her onto her mound of pillows and blankets.

'Then *I'll* have to answer for the consequences, Mike McTavish.' She smiled, and her eyes were wise with love and cherishing. 'I'll answer for the consequences for both of us. For ever and for ever and for ever.'

CHAPTER SIXTEEN

THERE was only one more time of waiting…

Somehow, by the time the twins woke in the morning, Mike and Erin were demurely dressed and ready to greet them with a real semblance of dignity. Mike refused Erin's offer of breakfast, gave her one long kiss of farewell—watched with avid interest by each twin—and then took his charges home.

As Mike lifted the twins into his car he turned and hugged Erin hard—and then held her away from him.

And a shadow fell over her bubble of happiness.

'I won't see you for a while, Erin,' he said briefly. 'I need…I need to do some hard thinking.'

And Erin was left with silence.

All that day Erin went about her work singing. Mike had said he needed to do some hard thinking—but surely…surely he couldn't escape the fact that they were destined for each other?

Could he?

It seemed he could.

What followed was nearly three days of silence. Not even the twins appeared for their riding lesson.

Erin telephoned on the second day, confused and unable to bear it, and the telephone was answered by Mike's foreman.

'Mr McTavish and the children are extremely busy,' Dan told her firmly. Was Erin imagining it or was there laughter in the foreman's voice? 'They'll contact you when they have a spare minute.'

There were seemingly no spare minutes.

And the joy started to fade.

Mike McTavish had said he loved her. Dear heaven, she'd thought he meant... She'd thought he'd meant to marry her.

Was she worse than a fool?

By the third day Erin was ghost-like, and there wasn't the least desire to sing left in her heart.

Jack O'Connell said nothing. He watched his granddaughter with knowing, concerned eyes and he kept his thoughts to himself.

Until that third afternoon. Tuesday...

Jack walked up to the mail box and came back holding a letter addressed to Erin in a child's scrawl. He watched as she tore it open—and watched as her white face flushed pink and then paled again.

'Well, lass?'

Erin's eyes flashed up to his—and she saw that Jack O'Connell was darned near as anxious as she was herself.

'Well?' he repeated.

'I'm...I'm invited to... I'm invited to dine at the McTavishes' tonight,' Erin whispered. 'Laura and Matthew and...and Mike request the pleasure of my company...' She broke off and stared down at the card.

The nightingales were starting up again all by themselves.

'What, aren't I invited, too?' Jack teased, and then at her look he chuckled and kissed her on the cheek. 'Get on with you, girl. I'm joking.' He hesitated. 'I notice no Caroline...'

'I don't think Caroline and Mike are getting married any more,' Erin said carefully, and watched Jack's face split into a grin of unholy enjoyment.

'Well, how about that? What are you waiting for, then, girl? Into your Sunday best and off you go.'

Erin's Sunday best still had toffee stains on it from an afternoon not so long ago spent with one collapsed *croque-en-bouche*.

Still, it was the best she could do. She dressed with care, left her hair hanging free and then took the truck to the McTavishes.

The invitation said six p.m. Erin made herself wait until two minutes past before presenting herself at the front door.

The front door was opened by Matthew.

Erin took one look and realized she was being treated to something very special. Matt was dressed to the nines, black trousers, white shirt and a bow tie that had clearly been lent by someone considerably larger.

'Good evening, Erin,' Matt said formally—and then giggled.

'Matt!' It was Laura's reproving voice from behind the door, and Matt recovered his dignity with an effort.

'Will you come this way?' he asked, and trod solemnly off towards the living room.

Bemused, Erin followed.

Mike and Laura were waiting to receive her.

The sitting room was spotless, as were both Mike and Laura. Laura was in a beautiful flouncy frock, with her hair beautifully brushed and adorned with a large pink bow—and for the first time in her life Erin saw Mike in a dinner jacket. All black and white and intensely formal—and intensely male.

It was all Erin could do not to gasp at the sight of him.

'Erin...' Mike stood and stretched out his hands, his eyes a caress in themselves—but Laura was before him. She reached out for Erin's hand and solemnly shook it.

'Good evening, Erin.' She smiled—the perfect hostess. 'We're so glad you could come. Could...?' She threw Mike a nervous glance. 'Could we offer you some sherry?'

'I'd be delighted,' Erin smiled.

And she was.

What followed was a dinner to end all dinners. Six courses in all—savouries, soup, entrée, sorbet, main and dessert. Each course was produced with the air of a solemn presentation, and Erin treated it with the attention and respect that was clearly expected.

After each course she was abandoned as Mike and the two kids headed for the kitchen. From behind closed doors she heard much clattering, splashing, giggling and the occasional crash and exclamation to match—but then the next course would appear with equal solemnity.

And then, after coffee and cheese, she was invited to inspect the kitchen.

Mystified, she rose and inspected.

The kitchen was spotless. Every dish had been washed and put away. It looked ready to start on the next dinner party.

'I…it's amazing…' Erin managed, trying not to appear mystified.

'That's not all,' Laura said importantly, and grabbed her hand. 'Now you have to come upstairs and look.'

Erin looked across at Mike—but Mike was watching Erin with almost as much anxiety as the twins.

And all four trooped upstairs as Laura, acting as self-appointed tour guide, pointed out beautifully made-up beds, neat piles of ironed clothes, tidy bedrooms…

'And a yellow stripe,' Matt told her breathlessly, pointing out a bright yellow stripe running all the way around the twins' bedroom. 'Look at our stripe. Caroline said a stripe was rid-ridiculous, but Laura told Mike I needed one and Mike said, "Let's do it." So Mike painted it yesterday. Just like Daddy did.'

Matt tucked his small hand into Erin's. 'And now it's just like home,' he sighed, and his hand held fast.

Just like home…

And then it was on to inspect the rest of the house. Polished floors, tidy bathroom, clean bath…

'Why…?' Erin took a deep breath as they reached the top of the stairs, the tour finally over. 'Can I ask why you're showing me all this?'

'Because,' Mike said solemnly, placing a hand on a

shoulder of each twin, 'Mrs Brown hasn't been here for three days.'

'For...'

'For three days we've done the lot ourselves,' Mike went on. 'We've dusted and polished and cleaned and ironed. We've read cookery books until we're practically master chefs. If you think tonight's dinner was a great meal, wait until you taste Matt's vegemite sandwiches! We have, in fact, thoroughly domesticated ourselves. Which brings us to what we would like to say to you.'

'Which...which is?'

'We want you to marry us,' Matt burst out, unable to contain himself any longer. His small face was pink with excitement. 'Mike says you can't do housework, and he says we need someone who can do housework or we'll be...we'll be a disaster area, he says, all by ourselves. So we all decided we'd learn. So now we don't need someone who knows housework at all, Erin. We need you.'

We need you.

Three absurdly anxious faces looked directly at hers. Erin looked from Laura—to Matt—and then finally up to the man causing all the trouble. The man standing looking at her with that damned smile that made her heart turn over.

'Does...does this invitation come from you too, Mike McTavish?' she asked breathlessly, and Mike's anxious face broke into a smile. He released the twins and took her hands in his—in a grip that said he'd never let go.

'With all my heart,' he said softly. 'But...but don't answer yet. Wait, Erin... There's more...'

'M-more?' She couldn't get past his eyes.

'Fetch the travel brochure, Matt,' Mike said, his eyes not leaving her face.

Matt scuttled away and was back in ten seconds flat— holding out a glossy crimson brochure.

'What...what is it?' Erin asked breathlessly, and those wonderful eyes laughed down at her.

'It's five open-ended tickets to the U.S.' Mike smiled. 'We thought… We thought your final quibble might be Jack. So, we did a couple of things. We wondered about combining households so we're one huge family—and we rang your parents in Pittsburgh after Jack gave us the number.'

'You rang my…?'

'Now, we didn't tell them you and I were getting married,' Mike informed her, ignoring her gasp. 'We just suggested it was a possibility. And we asked them— what if all five of us came to America for a nice long honeymoon?'

'Five…' Erin could hardly breathe. She could hardly think.

'You and me.' Mike touched each finger of his right hand in turn. 'Matt and Laura. And Jack. We thought, if you're agreeable, we'd take your grandpa to see his son.'

Erin swallowed. And swallowed again.

'Well?' Mike smiled. 'Well, our Erin?'

'You mean, take Grandpa to see Dad?' Erin breathed, finally able somehow to make her lips form the words. 'But, Mike…'

'Now, we don't want to force your hand,' Mike continued, the laughter behind his eyes giving the lie to his words, 'but your mother seemed to think that your dad wants to see his father more than anything else in the world. And she also suggested that while you and I went off and had a honeymoon—and your mom says the States is full of really special places for two people in love to have a honeymoon—we could leave Jack with your dad for a really long visit. Dan could manage both farms while we're away. And your mother… Well, she thought, if the twins liked, maybe she could take them to Disneyland.'

'Disneyland!' Matt and Laura yelled as one. 'Disneyland!'

'Now…' Mike somehow had hold of Erin, pulling her

in to nestle firmly in his arms. 'Now, you don't have to
say yes all at once, Erin, love. It's not like we're
pressuring you or anything.'

'No?'

'Disneyland, Disneyland!' yelled the twins.

'Would we pressure you?' Mike asked innocently, and
held her away at arm's length. 'Twins, we're not pressuring Erin, are we? If she wants to say no, then all she
has to do is say no. Isn't that right, twins?'

And they were all looking at her—the twins like anxious sparrows—and Mike's face was suddenly not all
that sure either.

And then Erin was laughing and crying all at once,
and trying to squeeze the whole three of them into her
arms at once—trying to fit all three close to her heart.

'Oh, you ridiculous…you crazy… I love you all so
much I think I'm going to cry.'

'Erin…' Matt's tiny voice whispered at waist-level.
He was hugging her around her hips almost as hard as
his uncle was holding her breast-high. 'Does that mean
you'll marry us?'

'It definitely does.' Erin smiled as Mike scooped her
up into his arms with a war-whoop of triumph. 'It definitely does, Matt.' She could hardly speak for laughing.
Or crying. And then she could hardly speak for being
kissed. She fought back—and Mike released her lips by
a quarter of a inch to let her get her words out. 'It surely
does, Laura.'

'And me too?' Mike demanded, his voice half-
laughing, half-serious. 'Me too, my darling Erin?'

'You too,' Erin told him tenderly, before his mouth
came down and possessed her again. 'It sure does mean
I'll marry you, Mike McTavish. With all my heart.'

MILLS & BOON®

Next Month's Romances

♡

Each month you can choose from a wide variety of romance novels from Mills & Boon. Below are the new titles to look out for next month from the Presents™ and Enchanted™ series.

Presents™

Enchanted™

Meet
A PERFECT FAMILY

Shocking revelations and heartache lie just beneath the surface of their charmed lives.

The Crightons are a family in conflict. Long-held resentments and jealousies are reawakened when three generations gather for a special celebration.

One revelation leads to another - a secret war-time liaison, a carefully concealed embezzlement scam, the illicit seduction of another's wife. The façade begins to crack, revealing a family far from perfect, underneath.

"Women everywhere will find pieces of themselves in Jordan's characters"
–Publishers Weekly

The coupon is valid only in the UK and Eire against purchases made in retail outlets and not in conjunction with any Reader Service or other offer.

- -